THE SICILIAN'S
RED-HOT
REVENGE

THE SICILIAN'S RED-HOT REVENGE

BY

KATE WALKER

⊙™ MILLS & BOON®
Pure reading pleasure

First published in Great Britain 2007
Large Print edition 2007
Harlequin Mills & Boon Limited,
Eton House, 18-24 Paradise Road,
Richmond, Surrey TW9 1SR

© Kate Walker 2007

ISBN 978 0 263 19490 6

This special book is dedicated to four
important writers in my life:

Marjorie Phillips, who created the first dark,
ambiguous hero I fell in love with

Mary Stewart, whose books inspired me to want to
write my own heroes as powerfully as she created hers

Dorothy Dunnett, whose complex heroes and amazing
storytelling have thrilled and absorbed me for years

Marguerite Lees, who believed in me from the start

CHAPTER ONE

EMILY sighed and kicked off her shoes, leaning back against the beach wall as she stared out at the blue-grey stretch of sea. The weak late-autumn sun shone down on her upturned face and the soft sand supported her comfortably. It was just so good to be still and on her own at last.

For the moment, all was silence—and peace. And it felt wonderful.

She sighed again, savouring the quiet around her, enjoying it after five long weeks of non-stop wretchedness. She thought she'd known what misery was like in the past, but this last month had shown her another sort of hell.

She had had to get away.

She couldn't have taken another moment of being stared at, talked about, with every last move she made the subject of comment and gossip.

And disapproval.

But here, at last, she could be on her own—be herself.

For now.

After the confines of the hospital, the space was wonderful. The air felt fresh and clean, touched with the exhilarating tang of ozone, and it was a delight after the artificially maintained temperature of the wards.

But best of all was the fact that no one was watching her.

'And I thought it was all over…'

Bringing her fist down on the sand with a thud, she snatched up a handful of the slippery grains, clamping them tight between her fingers and her palm, blinking fiercely to fight against the hot tears that stung at her eyes, blurring her vision. But then, with a fierce effort, she forced a new control on herself, shaking her head in both denial and despair.

Today was the day that she should have been free. The day when everything should have been signed and sealed, when it was all over and she could move on into a new life. Instead, she had been pulled back into the old one, with no hope of any liberation, no light at the end of the long, dark tunnel she was looking down.

'No…no. Let it go!' she commanded herself. *'Let it go.'*

And slowly, reluctantly, her fingers obeyed her, uncurling, opening, letting the sand slither through the openings between them to fall back onto the ground.

She only needed a day, she'd said. Just twenty-four hours before she would go back, face them all again. She knew her duty—and she would do it. But she just needed time to breathe.

The sound of the sea lapping against the shore brought her head round again, her eyes staring out at the distant horizon. The wide expanse of the ocean looked cool and inviting, calling to her in a way that nothing had done for so long. Living in the city meant that she hadn't been to the beach in …

In how long? Far, far too long. And she hadn't been paddling in the sea since she was a child. Life had closed in on her and Mark would never have countenanced seeing her indulge in anything so undignified and unrestrained.

But there was nothing to stop her now!

A whole new rush of enthusiasm flooded her thoughts, driving away the sadness and the tiredness of just moments before. With excitement pulsing in her veins she scrambled to her feet and set off down the sloping beach towards the water, moving slowly at first, then speeding up, breaking into a run, and finally racing full pelt down towards the white foam-topped waves as they broke upon the shore.

'Ooooh!'

The water was cold. Icy. Far colder than she had ever anticipated on a day like today. The shock of the chill against her skin was stinging, sharp, making her dance awkwardly, up on her toes, lifting first one foot and then the other out of the water, then letting them down again for the sheer thrill of the exhilarating sensation.

And suddenly it was as if the past days—the past months—had never been and she was a child again, free, uninhibited and laughing. Throwing her head back and opening her arms wide, lifting her face to the sun, she danced for sheer joy at the sense of freedom. Her blonde hair spun out around her face and the salty water splashed against the tight denim jeans she wore, soaking into the plain white long-sleeved T-shirt as she splashed, whirling round and round and laughing as she hadn't laughed in years.

It didn't matter if she looked like an idiot. She didn't care if she appeared as mad as a hatter—

because no one was looking. The beach was totally deserted from end to end. There was no one there. No one to see or hear her. No one to care.

No one was watching her.

He couldn't stop watching her.

On the deserted promenade, the tall, dark man stood, feet planted square on the paving stones, hands in his pockets, eyes narrowed against the sun, staring down at the woman on the beach before him.

He couldn't take his eyes off her.

He had spotted her from a distance as she drove the compact blue car down the hill from the town, travelling at just enough of a speed to draw his attention but not enough to be totally reckless. And even as he'd turned his dark head to watch she pulled up sharp against the kerb, yanking on the brakes and switching off the engine. Even from this distance he'd been able to see the brusque sharpness of every movement, the way that she had seemed almost to jump out of the car. She'd barely paused enough to slam the door and lock it before she'd been striding across the pavement, almost running down the worn wooden steps that led to the beach.

And just for a moment then he'd been really alarmed, a dark expression of concern creasing his forehead, drawing the jet-black brows together in a watchful frown. She seemed so distracted, so absorbed in something that was upsetting her, so close to some edge that every instinct had warned him to be wary—to watch more closely His long body had tensed, muscles tightening. He'd even been on his toes, ready to move—to run—if she was actually, as he had first thought—first feared—heading for the sea.

Was his imagination running away with him, or was she actually…?

But no. The breath he hadn't even been aware of holding in hissed from him in a sigh of release as he watched her march a couple of metres over the sand, slipping and sliding in its softness, and then throw herself down onto the ground, kicking off her shoes and lying back, her eyes closed.

But still he couldn't take his eyes off her. And he couldn't explain why. She was lovely, there was no question about that. Middle height, middle build, with a neat waist and curving hips. Her breasts were small and high as they pushed at the white cotton of the loose T-shirt she wore with rubbed and faded jeans. Her hair was pale blonde, cut neat, smooth and sleek, so different from the colouring and the style of the women back in Sicily where he lived.

So with her cool colouring would there come a temperament to match? If he approached her would she freeze in the so very English way that said without words, Do I know you? We haven't been introduced.

He didn't know but he was damn well going to find out. He couldn't turn his back, walk away, without ever having met her. From the moment he'd seen her, something about her had pulled at his senses, demanded attention. He had to meet her; had to look her in the face. Had to see if her eyes were blue or grey and he had to hear her voice…

But she was on the move again. Even as he started forward she had pushed herself up from her position on the sand and was running down the beach to where the sea lapped against the shore. Her feet slipped and slid in the sand, the movement made her hips press tight against the worn denim of her jeans, and the sway of her breasts made his mouth dry. He felt the clutch of hunger low down in his body reminding him of how long it had been since he'd been with a woman—too long. When he'd come to England, romancing had been the last thing on his mind.

He'd had enough of that with Loretta and the marriage she'd almost trapped him into. Even now the memory of her scheming and lying sent a cold sensation trickling down his spine. This time in England couldn't have come at a better moment. Here, he could forget about being Vito Corsentino and just be himself.

And until now just being himself had meant no women in his world or in his bed. Life was easier, less complicated that way…

But one look at this woman had changed all that.

Right now the thought of a woman—this woman—in his bed was the first thing on his mind. The only thing on his mind.

She was running headlong into the sea, dancing a little as the chill foam of the waves broke over her toes, waving her arms in the air like a small child suddenly released from its mother's hold. The salt water splashed dark patches on her jeans, dampened the white T-shirt so that it clung to the curves of her breasts, and watching her made a smile tug at the corners of his mouth. Did she know how uninhibited—how wild—how all-fired *sexy* she looked like that?

Hell—the smile wavered as desire kicked in hot and hard, making him shift uncomfortably. It really had been too long that he had been without a woman.

But all that was going to change.

Sweeping back the sleek black hair that the breeze from the sea had blown into his eyes, he headed for the steps down onto the sand.

He didn't know who she was or where she had come from. But tonight she was going to be his.

It was a good thing that no one could see her, Emily reflected as she skipped over the waves, dodging the little foaming eddies and splashing in the cool flowing water, feeling the sand suck at her toes as the tide pulled it forward and then back.

She hadn't felt this free—this uninhibited in years, not since she had met Mark Lawton and certainly not in the past eighteen months or so. But here, now, it seemed as if some of the burdens that had weighed her down had slipped from her shoulders, leaving her free and liberated at last. It was almost as if the years had slid from her too and she found herself giggling as the cold water tickled her feet, breaking over her ankles as she went in deeper.

She should have rolled up the hems of her jeans, to save them from getting damp, but quite frankly she didn't care. They were old, old and worn, and almost at the stage where she should have thrown them away—perhaps after this, when she finally found peace with herself, and peace with her life, she would do that.

But for now she didn't care if she got soaked to the skin. Jumping high, she landed with both feet, sending up another spray of the water in an icy splash, laughing as she stamped hard, wetting her jeans even more.

Oh, this was fun—kicking the water up before her, she danced further and further from the shore, heedless of the way that the sea soaked into the legs of her jeans, dancing, whirling spinning, the clear blue of the sky with its white puffs of clouds revolving round and round her until she felt dizzy. Her breath was coming in shaky, breathless gasps, laughter bubbling up inside her, as she turned faster and faster and…

'*Oh!*'

It was a cry of shock and panic. Already further out than she had expected, she hadn't realised that there was a sort of shelf at the edge of the sea, where the land fell away beneath her feet. Stumbling down it, she missed her footing, twisted her ankle, fell, shocking and hard, down into water that was suddenly up past her waist, her breasts.

She landed with a gasping splutter, tumbling head first into the chilly waves, feeling the sting of salty water break over her head, soaking into her hair.

'Oh, help!'

She had to get up. Had to get to her feet. But the current was stronger here, swirling round her, tugging at her clothes, dragging her down. The soaking jeans were heavy and clinging, the T-shirt drenched. Her hair was in her eyes and the sting of salt water made her blink hard, vision blurring, tears forming.

'Help!'

A real panic was setting in now. She scrabbled at the sand, felt it slip and slide away from her as she tried to push upwards to her feet. But just as she thought she was going to manage it, another bigger, fiercer wave thundered towards her, rearing up, the curves at the top frothing white and angry-looking, blotting out the sky. And at the same time the ebb of the tide beneath her tugged away the faint hope of a grip she was getting, knocking her back down again in a rush.

'No!'

It was a wail of despair, one that was silenced

shockingly, blotted out under the heavy fall of water that tumbled over her head, into her eyes, flooding her open mouth. Gasping and choking, she could only give in for the moment, letting herself be carried down, down, deep under the waves, tugged by the undertow, thrown up again to the top...

'*Help!*'

She was going to drown...going down again. What was it they said about the third time? Oh, dear heaven—please ...

She tried to snatch in a deep breath, hoping to hold it under the water, but only succeeded in inhaling more stinging, burning water, choking on it. She couldn't see, couldn't hear, couldn't...

'I've got you...'

The words came to her through the roaring in her head. She could only hear them as another, different sound, one she didn't really believe in because there couldn't be anyone else here, couldn't be someone who had come to her rescue, couldn't—

But then suddenly, just as she feared she was going to black out, something—everything—changed.

Impossibly—unbelievably—Emily felt strong hands grab hold of her, fixing tightly around her arms. She was caught, held, then hauled up, up, out of the water, her mouth opening wide on a gasp of shock and wonderful, pure, breathable air. The rush of it into her beleaguered lungs after the pressure of the water she had tried so hard not to inhale made her chest heave, cough, her thoughts spin. She was aware of the blue of the sky, clear and spotted with white clouds after the darkness of the water, but her eyes stung and her legs would not support her. Caught once again in the pull of the tide, she swayed weakly, almost fell.

The strong arms around her tightened even more. Changing position slightly so that they clamped about her waist and her chest, they pulled her up against something hard and warm and muscular.

Something—or rather, someone, hard and warm and powerfully male. The heat of him reached through her sodden clothes to warm her shivering body. The power of him surrounded her, supported her. She wasn't sure if the pounding in her ears was that of her own heart or his, only that it was hard and fierce, and, wonderfully, when she had come close to fearing the exact opposite, marvellously potent and alive.

'*Madre de Dio!*' The voice in her ear was rough

and raw, the accented words almost incomprehensible through her whirling thoughts. 'I feared I would not reach you in time. Are you all right?'

Was she?

Still unable to open her streaming eyes, or form coherent words, Emily could only nod silently, her thoughts further scrambled by the way that the movement brought her face close against the hard bones of a powerful shoulder, her senses tantalised by the ozone-tinged scent of his skin.

'OK…' she managed but knew that she was not yet ready to have him let go. Her feet barely touched the ocean bed, her toes simply drifting in the swirling sand, and she prayed that her rescuer wouldn't let her go, fearing she would be dragged away again with the ebb and flow of the white-capped waves.

But he showed no sign of even thinking about releasing her. Instead he pulled her up closer, moved his hands again. Before she could quite register what he had in mind, he had swung her up off her uncertain feet, his arms coming under her legs as he lifted her high out of the water.

'Ohhh…!'

Instinctively her own hands flew up, her arms fastening around his neck, holding on tight. She felt the muscles bunch in his shoulders as he took her weight, adjusted his stance, bracing strong legs against the powerful tug of the tide. Then, turning, he began the slow, difficult journey back to the shore, ploughing through the waves that still broke against them, spattering them both with cold spray.

'Almost there…'

Emily didn't know if he expected a reply. She couldn't give him one if he did; couldn't find the words. Her head was against his chest, the heavy, regular beat of his heart under her cheek.

If she opened her salt-crusted lids she could see the smooth line of his throat, the olive skin tanned gold even this late in the year. A slight movement of her head made it possible to see the point where his hair, jet black even without the soaking that the sea had given it, covered the bronzed skin at the nape of his neck. He wore his hair longer than most men she knew, the dark strands brushed against the neckline of his navy T-shirt, slightly unkempt, so very, very different from the tightly controlled, cropped way that Mark had always worn his.

But that was Mark. Everything about him had always had to be controlled. Except his drinking.

When he drank all sense of control went out the window, and a very different man took over.

'No!'

The word escaped her as she shook her head, trying to drive away the thoughts she didn't want. She had come here today to get away from all that and she was not going to spoil her hard-won freedom by letting unwanted memories intrude and upset her.

'No?'

The man who held her had heard her and his determined stride slowed, halted, his dark head turning, looking down at her. She saw the sudden flash of deep dark eyes, stunningly beautiful eyes fringed with impossibly long, luxuriant lashes, watched his black brows draw together in a frown.

'What…?'

'I'm fine…'

She didn't know what else to say. She didn't want him to stop; wanted to stay in his hold, in his arms like this forever. Or at least in the space that seemed to have reached out to enclose her like a bubble, suspended in time.

'You're sure?'

'Oh, yes, I'm sure—don't let me go.'

Had she really said that?

The water must have battered her brain more than she'd realised. She felt as if she'd completely lost touch with reality. Had she really just asked this man—her unexpected rescuer, the man who had scooped her up from the waves when she had felt that she was going to drown, not to let her go? To keep her in his arms?

But the truth was that in those arms she felt wonderfully safe, protected as never before. It was as if the broad shoulders that supported her, the chest against which her head rested, had come between her and the world, acting as a defence against the trials and disasters that had darkened her life over the past months. With those arms around her she could, if not forget about the disasters that she had run away from and the problems and situation that awaited her when, inevitably, she had to go back, then at least put them out of her mind.

'Oh, I've no intention of letting you go,' that wonderful rich, deep voice with the surprisingly lyrical accent assured her. Just the way that he spoke sent warm waves of sensation running over her skin, easing the cold of her drenching in the sea, warming her blood. 'Not until I'm sure that you can stand on your own.'

And most likely not even then, Vito told himself. He had hold of this woman now; he wasn't going to let her go.

His heart had barely stopped racing, hardly slowed from the moment he had seen her dancing wildly in the sea, her hair swirling round her face, arms waving in the air. But then there had been that pulse-stopping moment when she had seemed to stumble, when her hands had flown up into the air. She had spun on one leg, fallen—and the white-crested waves had crashed over her head.

He hadn't even been aware of moving, of racing down the strand to the sea. At some point he had kicked off his shoes and left them, careless of where they fell. His jacket had followed some-where and all the time he had been running, running through the sand, into the water…

When he reached the spot where he'd last seen her he'd thought he'd lost her, the sea had already closed over her head. But then he'd seen, in the depths, the swirl of pale hair, an even paler face; the white of her T-shirt. And he'd plunged into the water. Eyes struggling against the sting, hands reaching out, closing over her arms, dragging her close, lifting her up and out…

At first he'd feared he was too late. She was

terribly limp—too limp. But then she'd choked, coughed, and the air had rushed into her lungs on a huge, gasping sigh. Her head had fallen back against his shoulder, blonde hair splaying out across his chest.

And suddenly everything had changed.

She was cold and wet. He was cold and wet. But what he actually *felt* was a heavy, heated pulse that throbbed through every vein. The soft weight of her in his arms, made his own body tighten in hungry need and it was all he could do not to turn his head to hers and press a wild, demanding kiss on her parted lips.

But for now practicality was what mattered. Already the woman was starting to shiver in his arms. He had to get her to the shore, check that she had suffered no ill-effects from her accident. And so, gritting his teeth against the clamour from his inner senses, he turned and ploughed his way back towards the land.

'Don't let me go,' she said again. 'Don't let me go!'

Didn't she know that that wouldn't be the problem? That the thought of letting her go had never entered his head? From the moment he had first seen her arrive at the beach, he had been caught, entranced, and now that he actually had her in his arms there was no way he was going to let her go. Not without exploring what this whole thing meant. Not without taking this unexpected, fiery connection to the furthest limits possible.

'Oh, I've no intention of letting you go,' he said again, disturbing himself even with the intensity of the way it came out. So much so that he amended it hastily, adding some nonsense about wanting to see her on her feet first.

And why, when they finally reached the shore, when his feet were on solid land, with the sand firm beneath them, did he not act on that? Why did he not let her down, still holding her, still supporting her, waiting to see if she could stand up by herself?

Because his whole body, everything that was in him, rebelled at the idea.

He had her where he wanted her and he wasn't about to let go.

'We're here,' he said when she didn't appear to be about to stir either. Certainly she showed no sign of wanting to move but just lay in his hold as if she belonged there. *'Signorina...'*

That caught her attention, brought her head up. Her eyes—they were, he now saw, the softest, clearest blue, blue like the sky reflected in the sea—widened, looked straight into his.

'You're Italian!'

'Sicilian.'

'Oh...'

It was the last thing Emily had expected. When she had fallen into the cold, turbulent waters of the English Channel on a very English beach, she had never imagined that the man who had come to her rescue, like some knight of old racing to the defence of his lady, would be anything other than local. But now, looking up into his face, she saw that there was no way he could ever be taken for an Englishman. The olive-toned skin covering powerfully carved features, high, angular cheekbones, and the full, sensual mouth that now curved in a devastating smile, revealing white, white teeth, were definitely not the sort of looks she saw around her every day.

'Perhaps we should introduce ourselves. My name is Vito ...'

'Emily...' she managed awkwardly, her tongue stumbling even over her own name as she struggled with the over-heated race of her heart.

Those deep-set dark eyes burned down into hers with an intensity that seared her skin, making it flame with heat. It was as if the sun had suddenly come out from behind a cloud, almost blinding her, and she had to turn her head away, closing her eyes and burying her face in his shoulder.

She should say thank you, she knew. She should say *thank you for rescuing me and now would you please put me down? Let me stand on my feet…?*

But she couldn't do it.

She couldn't think straight, couldn't say anything.

The scent of his skin surrounded her. Warm and musky and still overlaid by the ozone from the sea. She took it in with every breath, felt it enfold her like the strength of his arms. No man had touched her, no man had held her in too long. No man except Mark, but Mark's hold had never affected her like this. Even in the beginning. Mark's arms had never felt so strong, his skin hadn't had that wild, intoxicating scent that went straight to her head like a swallow of the most potent of spirits, making her thoughts spin.

'Emily…'

That voice, that accent made her name into a totally different sound. They took away the clipped, essentially English, pronunciation she was so used to hearing every day and transformed it into a warm, lyrical sound, one that stirred her senses so that she nestled even closer, burying her face against Vito's chest, in the curve between his neck and his shoulder.

The warmth of his skin was against her cheek, the still damp strands of his hair brushing her ear as he moved his head, making her draw in a long, ragged breath. And with that breath she took in once more the essence of him, the scent of his skin, the taste…

In the warm, concealing darkness her closed eyes fluttered open, fixed on the point where just inches away from her, the heavy, regular throb of his pulse beat just under the skin. The firm stretch of olive skin was so smooth, so tempting… If she just moved her head…

It was only when her lips touched the warmth of his flesh that she realised what she'd done. And by then it was too late, way too late. Just the feel of it underneath her mouth, the taste of it on her tongue, was like a drug, making her blood heat, her senses yearn. Something hot and hungry and uncontrollable was uncoiling in the pit of her stomach, sending shivers of reaction along the pathway of every nerve. She couldn't stop herself from pressing her lips to that pulse again, breathing in the scent of his skin, tasting it with her tongue.

'Emilia,' Vito said again but this time on a very different note. One that matched the thunder in her head, the sensations in her body.

'Vito...' she breathed against his neck and slowly lifted her head, turning back towards him, tilting her mouth...

And found it taken in a sizzling, blazing kiss that sent reaction scorching through every inch of her.

CHAPTER TWO

THE world tilted, swung round her. Her vision blurred, her thoughts fled. Somewhere high in the sky above her, the cry of a lone gull was the only sound she was aware of, but it seemed to belong to another world, not the hot and hungry one that had suddenly reached out to enclose her, sweeping away all other sense of reality. And very soon even that faded, drowned out by the pounding of her own blood in her head.

She had let her arms drop from around Vito's neck but now she flung them back up again. Not for support but to draw his head down, press those seeking, demanding lips even closer to her own.

His arms no longer held her, or, rather, they still held her but in a very, very different way. The strength of his support had gone from under her legs, letting her slide down the hard, muscled length of him, until the tips of her toes brushed the sand, dangling just above the actual expanse of the shore. And this time one arm was clamped tight around her waist, crushing her to him, while with the other he laced hard fingers through the partly dried tangle of her hair, twisting slightly to hold her head just where he needed it, her mouth under his so that he could take what he wanted.

She was burning, softening, melting against him. She scarcely knew where her body ended and his began. And as he loosened his hold slightly so that she slid downward, over the long length of his powerful body until her feet were finally back on the sand, although not yet actually supporting her, that feeling intensified to almost agonising proportions. Her breasts were crushed against his chest, her hips cradled his pelvis, feeling the heat and pressure of his arousal hard against her. Her mouth was opening under his, allowing the intimate invasion of his tongue, tangling with her own, tasting the personal essence of him that had been on his skin and now was on her lips, on her tongue.

She had forgotten what this felt like. This instant, explosive, dramatic response to a man. The way that her heartbeat kicked hard, the way her breath came raw and uneven. She'd forgotten how it felt to know the honeyed burn of need, the heat pooling between her legs, making her writhe against his hard strength in hungry longing.

'*Emilia...*'

His version of her name was a raw breath against her mouth, his voice deepening and roughening until, she barely recognised it.

Recognised it!

The words echoed inside her head in a rush of shock and bewilderment. She had heard—what?—less than one hundred words from this man's mouth and yet she felt as if she knew his voice, would recognise it anywhere. It was as if that deep, husky sound, with the melodic accent she now knew to be Italian—Sicilian—was burned onto her mind like music etched onto a CD, so that she would always know it, always recognise it, no matter what happened.

It was as if it was part of her now, bound by links that could never be broken.

'Vito...'

She tried his own name, feeling it strange and exotic on her tongue. Just the sound of it sent a shiver down her spine, making her tremble in his hold.

How could this be happening to her? Just a few minutes ago she had arrived on this beach, not even knowing that this man existed, and yet now here she was, in his arms and…

The slam of a car door up on the promenade broke into the wild delirium that had invaded her brain, making her stiffen, pull her mouth away from Vito's. And in the same moment his handsome dark head came up, those deep black eyes suddenly blinking hard, losing the wild, unfocused look and staring down into her own wide blue ones with an expression that she knew must mirror her own.

What the hell am I doing?

He didn't have to say it, there was no need to speak the words out loud, they were written so clearly on his face, etched onto those stunning features.

And as soon as she saw that look, the same thought raced into her mind, slashing through the wild delirium that had clouded it, blurring her thinking and pushing her into actions that were so untypical of her usual behaviour.

What the hell had *she* been doing?

She didn't know this man. Knew nothing about him except his first name and the fact that he had just pulled her from what she had feared was going to be a watery grave—but she didn't *know* him! And yet she had been kissing him as if he was the love of her life. She'd been clamped so tight against him that they might have been one person, so close that there was no way she could have denied the sexual hunger he felt—or refuse to acknowledge the fact that it pounded through her own body too.

Anyone who might have seen them would have thought that they were already lovers, so intimate had been his hold on her, her response to him.

And this was a man that she knew precisely two facts about.

His name was Vito.

And he was a Sicilian.

It was mad. It was ridiculous. It was *dangerous*.

And it was as that last word exploded inside her head that she knew what had happened. She'd heard about it, read about it. She'd been in danger and this Vito had come to her rescue. The fear and the panic, the knowledge of danger and then the sheer, blinding exhilaration of having been saved. That had all created a wild, impossibly intense atmosphere. A hothouse atmosphere in which a very basic attraction had grown, been blown up out of all proportion and so created a volatile situation as a result.

Just the thought of it caught her body in a shiver

of response that made her tremble where she stood. Immediately those black eyes narrowed, sharpening perceptibly.

'You are cold! Forgive me—I should have thought.'

Already he was looking round, moving, heading in the direction of what she now saw was his jacket, discarded on the sand a short distance away, obviously in the haste of his mad dash to rescue her.

That thought should ease her mental discomfort, but instead it had the exact opposite effect, making her shudder even harder as reaction set in and the memory of just what had happened—what might have happened and how close she had come to it—attacked her nerves and made her quake inside, bitter tears of memory stinging at her eyes, her knees threatening to buckle beneath her.

This man—this darkly devastating, sexy, handsome man—had rushed into the turbulent water without hesitation when he had thought she was going to drown, throwing his jacket one way and the shoes she could now see further up the beach another. He'd come to her rescue when he had seen her going under for the third time, and no one had done anything like that, anything kind for her in a long, long time.

'Here…'

Vito was back at her side, swinging the jacket up and around her shoulders, pulling it closed at the front.

'This should help.'

'Th-thank you,' Emily managed, her tongue trembling as much as her limbs.

The jacket was comforting, so that she wanted to pull it closer, huddle into it to hide away from the world. But at the same time it started up a set of memories and emotions that in her present shocked state she was having terrible trouble controlling, so much so that the temptation to fling the garment from her and run was almost stronger than her need for comfort.

Almost.

Instead, she found that her fingers had clamped tight over the elegant lapels, crushing the expensive fabric ruinously as she clutched it to her like some sort of shield. Shock was setting in with a vengeance and she didn't know how to cope with anything.

'Are you OK?'

Idiota! Vito reproved himself furiously. Of course she was not OK! She had just almost drowned and now she was cold and probably in shock. What sun there had been earlier in the day was already fading rapidly, clouds gathering in the sky. Already some of those clouds were turning heavy grey and, if he was not mistaken, the storm that had been threatening all afternoon was now building up rapidly to breaking point.

And with the darkening of the skies had come a definite drop in temperature, a chill to the wind that had blown up. Instinctively he rubbed his own arms where the gooseflesh had already appeared. The damp jeans and T-shirt were cooling rapidly—and he wasn't half as badly soaked as Emily.

'*Idiota!*' he muttered again and saw those big blue eyes widen in shock and apprehension as she took a stumbling step backwards, away from him. Immediately his conscience reproached him savagely. With her blonde hair darkened by the water and tangled around her face, her skin pale and her lips almost colourless, she looked like nothing so much as a half-drowned kitten, one he had just kicked out at, hard.

'Not, not you—me', he assured her hastily. 'I should not be keeping you here talking when you're soaked through to the skin. You need to get inside—get warm—change your clothes. We have to get you home—where are your car keys?'

'Here…' She pulled them from her pocket, where, luckily, she had obviously put them before her wild dance in the water. 'But—but there's a problem…'

'There is?'

Vito had been turning away, heading for the promenade, but the comment and the shaky voice in which it was uttered brought him to an abrupt halt, swinging round to frown down at her again.

'What sort of problem?'

For a second he thought she was going to keep silent. The way she huddled closer into his jacket, avoiding his eyes, seemed to indicate that. But then she bit down hard on her lower lip and lifted her gaze to look him straight in the face.

'I—I don't live locally.'

'You don't?'

Emily shook her head, sending cold drops of sea water flying from her pale hair. 'I only meant to be here for the day—I was just passing through.'

No. His mind rebelled at the thought, rejecting it out of hand. That wasn't going to happen. She wasn't going to 'pass through', moving on and out of his life without a backward glance. He hadn't met a woman who had stirred his senses so fero-ciously in a long time—if ever. He wasn't going to just let her go without knowing what it would be like to take this instant, blazing attraction further. An attraction that she had felt too. He had sensed it in every inch of her body; felt it when she had trembled against him.

That hadn't been from cold, but from the exact opposite. The burning heat of desire that he'd experienced had made him shake too, but with need, with a hunger that he had been barely able to control. Its force had been primitive enough to bring him almost to the point of flinging her down onto the sand and indulging in the raw, primal need that they were both enduring. Only the knowledge that they were in such a public place had forced him to rein in the fierce desire that had him in its grip.

He still felt that way. But seeing the way she huddled into his coat imposed a control over his actions that warred cruelly with the still burning desire.

'But you have clothes in your car—something to change into…'

The words died on his tongue as she shook her head again.

'I didn't bring any with me. I—wasn't thinking straight.'

'Just passing through.' Vito repeated her words automatically, his mind busy.

'Just passing through,' she echoed and shivered again as a drip of water tumbled from her fringe and landed on her nose.

The small response made up his mind for him.

'Then you'll have to come back with me,' he declared, making it a statement of fact, not a suggestion. To him it was the only answer. There was no other way.

But Emily's blonde head tilted to one side, blue eyes studying him warily. And there was a new expression in them now. One that had suddenly reminded him that she might be just a kitten—but even the smallest cat had very sharp claws.

'Back where?'

'To my flat—'

He waved a hand in the direction of the far side of the seafront, vaguely indicating the general area of the small apartment he was renting for this year.

'You can have a shower, dry your clothes…' He saw her reaction in the way her face changed, even before she spoke. 'No?'

'No…' Her voice was low but firm.

'And why the hell not?'

He couldn't believe she was actually backing

out of this. He had been so sure that it was what she wanted too—almost as much as he did. This wasn't the same woman that he had held in his arms. The woman he had kissed.

Silently Vito cursed the fact that he had ever stopped kissing her—ever let her go. If he had just kept her in his arms, if he had clamped his lips to hers, sealed her mouth with his and carried her off the beach and down the road to his flat, then she would have gone without a word, he knew. The woman he had kissed had melted under his touch, yielding mindlessly and immediately, and he could have kept her that way—should have kept her that way. That woman would never have hesitated, never given him that wary, assessing stare. That woman would never have said no. He knew that without a doubt.

But he had let her go. He had given her a chance to pause and think and as a result she had drawn back. Something had changed her mind, stopped her from going with what she felt and making her act instead on careful, rational thought. And the heady, burning passion that had flared between them couldn't survive in the same atmosphere as careful, rational thought.

'I don't think that would be wise.'

'Wise!' He flung his hands in the air in a gesture of total exasperation. 'Wise! And you think being wise matters right now?'

He'd said the wrong thing. He could see it in the way her eyes sparked, the mulish, mutinous set to that neat chin.

'Common sense certainly does,' she said stiffly, all trace of that warm, responsive woman disappearing under a layer of ice. 'I know nothing about you! Not even your full name or—'

'Corsentino,' he inserted sharply as she drew a breath to go on. 'Vittorio Corsentino, usually known as Vito.'

'And is that supposed to mean something to me?'

'No.'

He was glad to see that it didn't. That there was no change in the expression in those soft blue eyes. There was no flicker of recognition and definitely not, *grazie a Dio,* any surfacing of the sort of acquisitive glint that had burned in Loretta's eyes when she had tried to press home her claim for support for herself and her unborn child.

'But you wanted my name.'

'And you think that's enough for me to let you entice me into your flat? You could be planning anything…'

'*Madre de Dio!*' Vito exploded. 'And why should I want to do you any harm? I rescued you…'

'You rescued me,' Emily flung at him. 'That doesn't mean you own me.'

'It does in some cultures,' Vito shot back. 'Save a life and it's yours to do with as you please.'

But that was just too much, Emily admitted to herself. It sounded too ruthless, too possessive, too much like Mark's gloatingly domineering, 'You can't leave me—you know you can't. Where would you go? How would you live?'

'Well, this isn't one of those cultures. And I am definitely not yours in any way.'

She wouldn't let herself think of the disappointment his reaction had created. Wouldn't let any hint of the pain that slashed at her register as she admitted that she had brought this on herself. She had been so stupid in reacting the way she had. In kissing him the way she had. Shock did weird things to the mind—and the body—and as a result she'd given this Vito quite the wrong impression. An impression it seemed he was determined to act on, while she was equally determined not to let him.

That all sounded fine and rational inside her head, so why didn't it quite ring true? Why couldn't she convince herself that this was truly what she meant?

Why was there still a tiny bit of her, a weak, emotional bit of her, that fought against the sensible, rational approach? That yearned for this to be more than that—to mean more than that? A yearning that made her fight to control her voice as she continued.

'I'm grateful to you for your help, obviously, but that's it. There's nothing else that need concern you.'

'I don't think so.'

Would the wretched man never listen? Why didn't he just give in and walk away? She was really beginning to feel the after-effects of the fright and the icy soaking she'd endured and it was a struggle to stay on her feet, never mind *argue*. All she wanted was to run to her car, get in and lock the door against the world. There, she could rest her aching head on the back of the seat, close her eyes and let the world go away. That was what she had wanted when she had first arrived. To switch off and let the world go away.

It was a cruel irony that she had only come here today to be on her own—get away from the problems at home—to escape from all the fights and the arguments that had been her life for as long as she could remember. She had wanted some peace and quiet which was why she had headed towards the sea. And she had thought she'd found it.

Until Vito Corsentino had appeared on the scene.

Until he had taken her in his arms and kissed her senseless.

Exactly—*senseless!* He had kissed her until she had lost what little remained of her mind. Until she had reacted in the most stupid, irresponsible way possible. So Vito Corsentino had affected her as no man had done for years. So he'd woken the secret, sensual part of her that had been buried, hidden away for so long. So his kisses and his touch had left her wanting more—she wasn't going to give in to that need. The results would be far too complicated—dangerous—destructive. She didn't want to get tangled up with anyone— least of all a man like Vito Corsentino.

'I want you to think so!'

She aimed to make her tone emphatic but the effort she was putting into stopping it from shaking at the same time only succeeded in making it sound harsh and brittle, colder than the waves that still broke against the shore near their feet.

'I appreciate what you did for me, and I thank

you for that, but I don't need anything more. And I definitely don't want to go to your flat—or anywhere with you! What I need—what I want—is for you to leave me right now. Just turn—walk away…'

For an uncomfortable, worrying second or two she thought he was going to argue further. She saw the flash of rejection in his eyes, watched that beautiful mouth harden and thin, his face losing all warmth, becoming as hard and fierce as the face of some wild hunter just as it scented its prey. But then, just as her heart quailed inside her and she struggled to find the strength to face another argument, to fight him further—to fight herself further and deny the weak, disappointed clamour of her own senses that were trying to tell her it didn't have to be this way—he suddenly, and totally unexpectedly, gave in.

'Fine.'

He threw up his hands in a gesture that in another man might have been meant to express defeat but even on such short acquaintance she knew that defeat was something this man would never acknowledge. Instead, he was revealing total exasperation, and dismissing the argument as not worth bothering to take any further. He'd had enough of this, his body language and the dark, glowering scowl he turned in her direction said. Enough of this and enough of her.

So he did as she'd asked, or, rather, demanded. He turned on his heel in the sand, sending the fine grains spraying up around his legs with the determination of the movement. And he walked away.

So now she'd got what she wanted. She'd got what she'd said she needed. So why didn't she feel as if that was what had happened? Why weren't her shoulders relaxing, her heartbeat easing as she watched him move away from her? Why didn't she feel glad—or at least a sense of release—at the way that every line in that tall, powerful body, the way that the long, straight back was held, the set of the broad shoulders, spoke of rejection and dismissal so that it was obvious that he wasn't going to reconsider or even hesitate? It couldn't be clearer that he had no intention of changing his mind, of turning back. And that was what she'd wanted; wasn't it?

So why did she feel a thickness in her throat, a knot around her heart, as if she was in danger of losing something valuable? Something she would regret discarding so carelessly in the future?

She watched him stride further up the beach to

where his shoes had been kicked off in that wild, frantic run towards the sea. To rescue her. As he stooped to snatch them up, still not giving the slightest glance backwards in her direction, her conscience twisted sharply inside her, giving a nasty little stab of reproach that made her wince inwardly. She shifted awkwardly from one foot to another on the soft sand, huddling closer into the jacket as a cold wind coiled round her, the black clouds now scudding across the sky, darkening the atmosphere threateningly.

The jacket! Her conscience stabbed at her again, more cruelly this time. Vito Corsentino had come to her rescue without hesitation. He'd dragged her from the waves and brought her safely to dry land. He'd even given her his jacket to keep her warm and to cover her sodden, bedraggled clothing and all she'd done was to tell him to go and leave her alone.

Had she even thanked him properly? What sort of an ungrateful idiot was she?

'Wait!'

He hadn't heard her. Or he'd heard her but he wasn't prepared to stop.

She watched his long, determined stride cover the sand, taking him further away from her with each movement... He would soon be out of earshot.

'Wait—please!'

One more stride further away. And another. But then, with this last one, he slowed, stopped, swung round. He didn't say a word but those dark eyes flashed the question *Well?* in her direction with a fierce impatience that made her heart quail inside her.

'Your jacket...'

She was shrugging herself out of his coat, coming forward, holding it out to him.

'You need it back.'

For a moment he stayed where he was, looking deep into her eyes, and then, briefly, that black-eyed gaze flicked down to focus on the garment she held towards him.

The hand he used to gesture expressed such total contempt that it was a dismissal of her as well as the apparently unwanted jacket.

'Keep it,' he said. 'You need it more than I do.'

'But...'

But Vito was already turning away again, even as she tried to form the protest.

'Keep it,' he tossed over his shoulder at her. 'It's getting cold and you have nothing else to keep you warm. I would hate to think that my efforts to save you from the sea would all go to waste because you caught a chill as a result.'

The memory of his rescue—the way that he had dashed into the sea without a thought—stung at her conscience again, making her shift uncomfortably on the sand, tracing a pattern in it with one bare toe.

'Vito, please don't do this…' she began again. 'I'm sorry—I—'

But what she had been about to say was drowned, totally obliterated, as with a roar of thunder and a brilliant flash of lightning the storm that had been threatening all afternoon broke suddenly and violently right overhead.

'That settles it!'

At least that was what she thought that Vito said but the truth was that she saw his lips move and barely caught any sound from them. This time it was the rain that swept away any hope of hearing properly, the heavens opening and a savage downpour thundering onto the sand, taking just a second to drench them all over again.

'Vito!'

His name was a cry of shock and confusion as once more water lashed against her face, drove into her eyes. Gasping and spluttering, Emily lifted her hands to cover her face, providing a little, inadequate cover, then just as swiftly let them drop down again as she realised that she was holding Vito's expensive and now very much worse-for-wear jacket up too.

'Oh, I'm sorry!'

But Vito didn't hear her or if he did, he didn't care. The next moment she was grabbed, those strong hands clamping hard on her again as once more she was swung off her feet and up into his arms.

'Damn the jacket!' he muttered roughly, inclining his head so as to dodge another battering from the rain. 'I told you it didn't matter. We'll talk about it when we get inside.'

'Inside where? I told you…' Emily began, only to have the words die on her lips as Vito glared down into her rain-swept eyes.

'And I told you that we'd talk about this *inside!*'

He was moving as he spoke, carrying her off the beach and climbing precariously up the steep wooden steps to the promenade. And all Emily could do was fling her arms around his neck and hold on tight, her heart in her mouth with the fear they might fall making her shiver even more than the storm that buffeted them ferociously. Vito had to pause a couple of times, rebalance himself, but he made it safely to the top of the steps and onto the security of the paved promenade.

'All right—you can let me down now!' Emily tried again but he simply shook his head, jaw set hard, dark eyes shuttered against her.

'I'm not letting you go until we're inside. We need to talk and we can't talk in this. I've saved you from drowning once—I don't intend to do it again. Like it or not, you don't have any choice— you're coming home with me.'

CHAPTER THREE

'ALL right, we're inside…'

Emily's voice was cold and tight, seeming even more stiff and hostile in the sudden silence that had descended after the door to the flat had slammed behind them, shutting out the slashing rain and muffling some of the sound of the storm that was still raging outside.

'So put me down—you promised!' she insisted when Vito hesitated, tempted not to go along with what she wanted.

It was her tone that set his teeth on edge. The sharp, peremptory edge to it had him clenching his jaw tight shut on the angry retort he was tempted to make, the equally abrupt refusal to do anything of what she wanted.

But there was another reason, of course. One he was less willing to acknowledge.

He didn't want to let her go. She felt good in his arms, in spite of the fact that she was still soaking wet, drops of water from her sodden hair dripping onto to him with uncomfortable regularity. But then he too was drenched, so he couldn't actually get any wetter. And he didn't want to put her down. He knew what would happen if he did. Then she would forget all about the flame of passion that had flared so wildly between them. She would put up the barriers, slam mental doors in his face, and it would be once again as it had been out there on the beach.

She would fight him every inch of the way, her pretty face stiffening, closing up, as it had done when he had suggested that she came back here. Well, he had her here now, but she was still fighting, and if that mutinous look on her face was anything to go by then her grip on her temper was fraying rapidly.

'Signor Corsentino…' she said warningly, and, deciding that, for now, cooperation was probably the best policy, he let her slide to the floor, as he had earlier let her slip down until her feet were in the sand.

And just as it had then, the slow slide of her body against his made him clench his jaw against the burn of sensuality that flashed through his body, the throb of hot blood in his veins. He had to fight against the impulse to grab her again and kiss her hard as he had done on the beach. But he knew that if he did that then she would fight him even harder. And fighting was not what he had in mind. So for now he'd play things her way—but only for now.

'I told you it's Vito,' he said, the tension between his mind and his body making the words harsh and rough.

'And I told you, I didn't want to come here, but did you listen?'

Did she know that she still looked like a half-drowned kitten, spitting and snarling at him like that? Her blonde hair fell in ragged spikes around her face, plastered to her cheeks by the rain. If she had worn any make-up then it had been washed away, but her long, thick lashes were clumped together with the rain, surrounding eyes that seemed as clear and blue-green as the sea beyond the promenade. And they were every bit as cool, no warmth easing the distant, considering look she had turned on him.

'So you'd like to leave?'

He decided to call her bluff.

The hall doorway was just behind him. All he had to do was to reach out, turn the handle. And, as luck would have it, just as he pulled the door open another crash of thunder sounded directly overhead and the rain pounded down again. A rush of cold air flooded into the confined space as Emily took a cautious step forward, looking even more catlike than before. But this time she was a wary, uncomfortable feline. One that shivered at the thought of facing the unpleasant elements outside.

'I thought not.'

With one foot he kicked the door to again, noting that this time she didn't even try to fight him on it.

'But what am I going to do?'

'Stay here at least until the worst of it passes over.'

'Thank you.'

Still not fighting him; that was progress. He walked across the hallway, opening the door into his living room, deliberately not looking to see if she followed him as he spoke again.

'And I think we'll both feel better if we have something warm to drink and get out of these wet clothes.'

'I don't have anything to change into…'

Unexpectedly, she was right behind him. So close that he could feel the warmth of her breath on the back of his neck. Swiftly he wheeled away, putting some distance between them as he turned.

Not quite enough, but then he could have been at the far side of the room and he would still have felt the sexual tug that linked his body to hers.

'I'm sure I can find you something—even if only a T-shirt. You can't stay in those things much longer.'

Not if he was going to have any hope of controlling his libido. In the hallway, with the heavy skies draining all the light, it had been too dark to see the way that the thin white cotton of her T-shirt had been turned almost transparent by the soaking it had received. Now here, with what light there was coming in through the big bay window, he couldn't be unaware of the way that it clung to the soft curves of her breasts, the slender shape of her ribcage. The faint pink of her skin showed through the wet material, seeming to tint it lightly.

Vito curled his fingers tightly into his palms, clenching them against the impulse to peel that T-shirt from her, reveal the smooth reality of the flesh underneath it.

'You could take a shower.'

He didn't care that it came out brusquely, that his voice sounded rough.

'The bathroom's through here…'

The way that Vito waved at the door was a blatant gesture of dismissal, Emily realised. He wanted her out of here—and out of his way. What had happened to 'we need to talk'? Or even to 'you don't have any choice—you're coming home with me'?

But the truth was that she was beginning to feel cold and uncomfortable again. The clinging white T-shirt was chilled and clammy and the wet jeans rubbed at her legs with every movement. The thought of that shower was wonderful—tempting—but along with it came the thought of going into this man's bathroom, stripping off…and that was what was making her hesitate. The action seemed too revealing, too intimate—and not just in a physical way. She hadn't been alone with a man, apart from Mark, for three years, and to contemplate being naked in Vito Corsentino's flat, even behind a closed door, seemed somehow so shocking that it made her legs tremble, and froze her into foolish indecision.

'Look, *signorina,* if you're not getting cold then I am.'

Vito had obviously come to the end of his limited patience and the way the sentence was forced from between gritted teeth, and a tight jaw, was a warning that he was not prepared to wait for very much longer.

'I am also trying to be a gentleman here by offering you the use of the shower first. But if you prefer to stand there looking like a drowned rat then could you at least move into the kitchen instead of dripping on my landlord's carpet?'

'Oh—I'm sorry!'

His tone stabbed at her, making her take several steps towards the door that he'd indicated, then pause, looking back guiltily at the water-darkened spot on the dull green carpet.

'If there's any damage—' she began but Vito didn't let her finish.

'I'll deal with it,' he declared brusquely, his impatience almost getting the better of him. 'If you'll just get into that shower!'

'Of course.'

The edge on his voice made her jump.

'There's no need to shout—I'm going.'

She fled through the door and let it slam closed behind her, coming to a halt in the middle of the room as she realised where she was and paused to survey her surroundings.

Not the bathroom. At least, not immediately, though another door on the far side of the room must obviously lead to that. Instead she was in a bedroom.

In Vito Corsentino's bedroom.

It couldn't be anything else. The relentlessly masculine atmosphere was there in the plain white walls, the denim-blue linen on the big bed.

The big double-bed.

'Oh, stop it!' Emily spoke aloud to herself to reinforce the instruction. She couldn't believe the thought that had flashed through her head, the way that even before she had realised it she had been looking more closely around the room, looking for evidence of the fact that Vito lived here alone. That there was no woman in his life.

Well, if there was a woman in his life then she clearly didn't live here. There was no sign of any feminine influence in the room. No cosmetics, no flowers, the only ornaments several dramatic and beautiful carvings in polished wood that stood on the dresser and the windowsill. Everything else was stark and had a strange temporary look about it, and the wardrobe door hung open, revealing only male clothing stored inside.

Male clothing…

A sudden shiver of discomfort slid down Emily's spine as it dawned on her that she still held Vito's jacket—the jacket he had taken off and put round her shoulders to keep her warm. Reluctantly, guiltily, she looked down at it, a gasp of horror escaping her as she saw the mess that the sea, the weather, and finally her own careless grip had made of the garment. It was hopelessly crushed, little more than a rag. It was ruined.

And the worst thing was that now that she had a chance to look at it, it was of far better quality than she would have ever expected when she looked round at the place that Vito lived in.

No…

Emily shook her head, looking round the room again. It was the flat that was the surprise. Somehow the small, slightly shabby ground-floor apartment didn't fit with the powerful, dynamic man that Vito Corsentino appeared to be.

But the jacket did.

And she'd ruined the jacket.

Her conscience was getting more uncomfortable by the minute. She was going to have to apologise—offer to pay to replace it.

But first she was going to get into that shower.

Carefully placing the jacket on the back of a nearby chair, smoothing the dreadful creases as best she could in the vain hope that the worst of them would hang out, she hurried into the bathroom.

She'd be as quick as possible. Just warm herself up, get back out there, talk to Vito and—

'Oh, no!'

Her thoughts trailed off on a yelp of shock and horror as she confronted her image in the mirror and recoiled from what she saw.

She looked a fright.

The wet, grubby clothes she had been prepared for, and the sodden hair. She hadn't been wearing any make-up—the need to escape, get away as fast as she could had meant that she hadn't even paused to smooth on her usual tinted moisturiser and add a slick of mascara to darken her fair lashes—but even so the pallor of her skin was shocking. And her hair!

Some of it still hung in rats' tails around her face, clinging to her skin and dripping cold, wet drops onto her cheeks. The rest had already started to dry and was bunched into salt-crusted lumps, sticking out at right angles to her head.

Suddenly the need to be in the shower sprang from more than wanting to warm up. Scrambling out of her clothes, she flung them into a corner, turned on the shower, switching the control to 'Hot'.

It was only when she was under the shower rose, with the water pounding down on her head, that she let herself relax enough to think again.

She'd looked like that and Vito had still kissed her!

Grabbing a bottle of shampoo from the side of the bath, Emily poured some into her hand and began to rub it over her hair.

Mark had always been so quick to point out her shortcomings, and to criticise if she had been looking anything but her best. He had always insisted that she was smart, elegant and beautifully groomed. Several times he had sent her back to their room to change if she had appeared in some outfit that didn't meet with his approval. He would have burst a blood vessel in fury if she had ever appeared in public looking like this!

Vito had seen her looking at her worst, hair a ragged mess, face pale—and he'd still kissed her! She could hardly believe it.

But she could *remember* it.

And as the warmth of the shower seeped into her chilled body she felt those memories flooding back along with it. If she closed her eyes then the fingers massaging her scalp weren't hers but Vito's hard, strong fingers that had closed in her hair, cradling her head as his mouth plundered hers. The warmth of the water playing over her skin was his touch, his caresses moving over her body, his hands soaping her breasts, sliding down her stomach…lower.

The pine-scented shower gel that was the only thing she had available filled her nostrils, making her feel that she was inhaling his scent, the personal signature of his skin. Her senses heated in a way that had nothing to do with the returning warmth to her body, her mind swimming in heady reaction. And in her ears the sound of the water was the crashing of the waves onto the shore, waves that seemed to underline rather than drown out the sound of a husky, softly accented voice speaking her name in a very special, totally unique way.

Emilia…Emilia…

Emily spluttered as she realised that she had actually sighed, swallowing some more water—warm this time. She snapped her eyes open, struggling to focus for a moment.

What *was* she doing?

Fantasising about Vito Corsentino—a man she had known for barely an hour!

Switching off the water in a rush, she reached for a towel. The single one available was far from generous and, once she had rubbed the worst of the moisture from her hair, she had to struggle to knot it around even her slender figure.

Perhaps there was another one or perhaps a robe

in the bedroom. Cautiously she opened the door, peering round it nervously.

'Emilia…'

It was the voice she had heard inside her head. The same husky tones, the same beautiful accent. But this time it was not her imagination that formed the sound. This time the tall, devastating form of Vito Corsentino was standing right in front of her, in the middle of the room, the towel she needed in his hand. He'd discarded his T-shirt somewhere so that the taut, muscled lines of his chest and ribcage and the gleaming bronzed skin lightly hazed with crisp black hairs were exposed to her hungry gaze, and those deep dark eyes of his were fixed on her as she hovered in the doorway.

And the look that burned in their black depths told her that she was in real trouble.

Vito had determined that he would stay well away from the bathroom. He would make the hot drink he had suggested, and concentrate on that. Take the opportunity to get his thoughts—and his libido—back under control. So he wanted this woman—that didn't mean he was going to rush into this like some horny adolescent who'd just discovered what girls were about.

He had her here; that was what mattered. She'd almost got away from him, so much so that he'd had to call her bluff, but now she was in his home and going nowhere for a while. He could afford to relax and start to enjoy this.

He surveyed the damp patch Emily had left behind on the carpet, a wry smile curling his lips. If there was any damage it wouldn't show, he reflected cynically. The whole carpet was so drab and old that a little more fading, another mark here or there would hardly matter. And if it did, he would buy the landlord a brand-new carpet—for the whole of the flat. It needed it.

The smile twisted into a grimace as he surveyed the small, shabby room with its old-fashioned furniture. It was a far cry from the large, white-painted Villa Limoneto he owned back home in Sicily, and the one time that his brother Guido had seen this flat he'd been stunned and disbelieving.

'You live here? Surely you could have found somewhere more comfortable—a little more spacious.'

'I don't need spacious,' Vito had laughed. 'There's only me. And I like being so close to the sea. Besides, there's the yard at the back where I can work on carving.'

It was the way he'd wanted to spend this year.
The year that was supposed to be his gift to
himself. The gift that he and his brother had
agreed on to mark their thirtieth year—twelve
months of freedom to be themselves. Twelve
months away from the pressures and discipline of
running the huge Corsentino Marine and Leisure,
the company they had built up between them.
Guido had spent his year in America, working as
a photographer, indulging his interest in that skill;
Vito had spent the last eight months in England.

So now, trying to see the small apartment
through Emily's eyes, he knew that it reflected
nothing of the truth about him. And that was
something that gave him a great deal of satisfaction. Just the way that out there, on the beach, he
had appreciated the way that she had simply
accepted his name, and he hadn't needed to fill her
in on anything more. So now he found he liked the
thought that she would only respond to him as a
man and not as someone with a fortune and an
international reputation behind him.

That had been Loretta's only concern, he
recalled, scowling now as he pulled off the T-shirt
that had become uncomfortably cold and clinging,
tossing it in the washing machine in the small

kitchen before heading to the sink to fill the kettle with water. It had been that reputation, that fortune she had been interested in. He had a whole new sense of release knowing that this time, for now at least, it didn't matter.

From the bathroom he could hear the sound of running water and knew that Emily had finally got into the shower. That was something that wasn't so great about the flat being so small. He didn't want to think of her standing in the shower, stripped naked, with the hot water sluicing through the fine blonde hair, pounding down on her skin, turning that creamy pale flesh pink with warmth as the heat flooded through it.

'Dannazione!'

He swore savagely as the coffee he had been aiming for the cafetière missed the glass jug completely and spilled all over the kitchen worktop. He didn't want to think about that!

But of course, having started imagining, there was no way he could force himself to stop. The erotic images flooded his head, swirling around in a way that made him grit his teeth against the temptation that burned up his body, twisted in his groin.

All he could hear was the sound of rushing water.

All he could smell—well, he would have sworn he could smell it even from here—was the scent of soap and shampoo and…

Hell, no! The flat was small but it wasn't so small that he could smell the warm female body underneath the soap, the hair that was being washed by the shampoo.

Coffee. That was what he needed.

Coffee would at least warm him up—fill his nostrils with another, completely unfeminine scent—distract him. *Madre de Dio,* he prayed it would distract him.

It was as the kettle boiled that he remembered he hadn't put out fresh towels, or found anything for Emily to wear. The way he was feeling, it would be better if she was clothed— at least for a while, he told himself, heading for the bedroom.

Inferno. All he knew about her was her name— and then only her first name. She hadn't even given him her surname.

There was a clean T-shirt in the dresser. A shirt to go over it in the wardrobe. And there were brand-new, unworn boxers still in the packet…

It was as he had them in his hand that he heard the water switch off.

And the fantasy in his head froze him to the spot and kept him there.

Emily, stark naked and dripping wet, stepping out of the shower and onto the grey-tiled floor of the bathroom. She would rub the towel over her face, along her limbs…

'Asciugamano…!' She'd need another towel.

Pulling open another drawer, he grabbed two towelling sheets from it, painfully aware of the silence beyond the door. A silence that tugged at his nerves, tangled in his gut. And then there was another sound, one that twisted even harder. He turned slowly—so slowly—and watched the door open a crack—then wider.

And it was worse than he had imagined.

The thin navy-blue towel was pulled tight around her body, constricting her breasts so that they were crushed against her chest, the lush, pale curves of them spilling out above the dark blue cotton. It barely covered one third of her body, exposing the soft curves of her shoulders and long, slender legs, curving down to fine, narrow feet, the small toes curling tightly and then straightening again. Elsewhere her skin was pink with warmth, her blonde hair darkened as it clung to the fine shape of her head. Her eyes were big and luminous, stunningly beautiful, her lashes clumped together by the water once again.

'Emilia…' he said, not caring that he gave away the dark sensuality of his thoughts in the way that he spoke.

'Vito…' His name was just a breath on her lips and as the sound died away, her soft pink tongue snaked out as she moistened her mouth.

The faint sheen that the gesture left behind was a temptation in itself. He found himself longing to move forward, put his hand under her chin, tilt her face up to his and kiss it away from her mouth. He could almost taste it in his imagination and his own mouth dried at the memory of how those lips had felt under his out there on the beach. His body hardened, hunger burning in his groin, making him clench his teeth against the sensation of hot need.

'I brought you towels…' He spoke abruptly to distract himself from his thoughts.

'Thank you.'

Her voice sounded deeper than before and there was a strange little husky note in it as if she had a raw throat from speaking too long or too loudly. And because he was looking straight into her face he saw the sudden change in her eyes, the way that they seemed darker and deeper than ever before.

And seeing it started a slow burn licking along his veins, heating his blood.

'*Niente.*'

'I—um…'

Emily could feel the heat rising over her exposed skin and up into her face as he held out the bundle of towelling towards her. Just how did she take the ones he offered her without actually letting go of the one she was wearing?

She couldn't let go. If she did then the towel that barely covered her would come undone; already it was only staying fastened because she was holding it pinched between her fingers and thumb. If she so much as breathed more deeply then it threatened to open wide, sliding down her body, exposing her nakedness underneath.

And with Vito looking at her like that then she already felt naked enough. Actually being naked was not something she wanted to risk.

Or did she?

'Could you—could you help?' she managed, speaking sharply to cover the unexpected twist of discomfort at the way her mind had thrown the unwanted question at her. The truth was that she didn't recognise the woman she had become since Vito had made his dramatic appearance in her life.

Even being here like this was rocking her sense of reality dangerously.

Those burning dark eyes took a moment to move from the way they had locked on to her but when they did she saw him sum up the situation in a second.

'*Scusi...*' he said, coming towards her at once, shaking out the larger of the two towels.

With a movement that reminded her instantly of the way that he had draped his jacket over her on the beach, he swung the towel like a cloak around her back, bringing it forward and under her arms. With his eyes fixed on hers, he held it taut at the front, leaving just enough room for her to wriggle out of the inadequate, already sodden towel, letting it drop to the floor while she was still totally covered by the newer, larger one he had provided.

'Thank you...'

It was uneven, breathless, and she knew that she was trembling, not from fear but from reaction to the way that the backs of his hands were warm against the sensitive skin of the tops of her breasts as he held the towel secure.

'*Niente...*' he said again but there was a rough-ness on the word that told her he was every bit as aware of the intimate contact as she was and that he felt exactly the way she did.

Hoping to improve matters, to ease the dizzying thud of her heart, she slid her hands into the top of the towel, tugging it closed and tucking in one end to fasten it across her breasts. But as an attempt to defuse the situation it was a total failure. In fact it just made matters worse.

Those strong, lean hands still lingered at the spot where the towel ended and her flesh began, their olive-toned skin looking very dark against the paleness of her own. And without the towel to hold, the broad tips of those long fingers rested right on the spot at the base of her throat where her pulse beat a hard, uneven tattoo, betraying the way she was feeling, the effect that just his touch was having on her. The skin of his fingers was un-expectedly hard and slightly rough, faintly abrasive on her flesh; not the touch of a man who spent his days at a desk, pushing only papers or working at a computer.

'The—the shower was wonderful.'

She stumbled over the words, knowing she was only using them to fill the silence, then wished she hadn't spoken when she saw the way his black-eyed gaze dropped to fix on her lips, watch them intently as they moved. Her throat felt closed and tight, her mouth painfully dry, and she swallowed hard to relieve it.

And saw him swallow too as if in response.

Why didn't he speak? Surely he should say something—*anything*. One of them had to create a conversation that would shatter this spell that seemed to have enclosed them, to bring them back to reality, break into the almost hypnotic trance that held them there. So still.

So close to each other.

So close, with Vito's hand on her skin, his hot gaze on her face, the heavy, thudding beat of his heart seeming to echo hers as it pounded in her ears.

'Vito...'

'*Si, carina?*' It was the softest of murmurs, a sound that was almost a caress in itself, and she could feel the warmth of his breath on her skin, on the curves of her ear, he was that close. 'What is it?'

What is it?

Emily's eyes closed as she fought with herself, with her deepest, most primitive female needs. This wasn't wise. It wasn't safe. What was that saying about fools rushing in?

'I—I...'

She should tell him to move away. To stop touching her. She had to tell him. But, oh, she didn't want him to move away. And she most definitely didn't want him to stop touching her.

But with her eyes closed she felt the touch of that hand on her collar bone with a new and sharper intensity. She knew its warmth and the unique combination of the softness of his skin and the rasp of those work-roughened fingers. With her eyes closed she could smell the warm male scent of his body, overlaid still by the tang of the sea.

The sea!

That thought and the memory it brought had her eyes flying open at once, locking at once with the darkness of his gaze. She couldn't look anywhere else, but she could touch, and when she reached out a hand that shook with a mixture of tension and awareness, the moment that it made contact with him, resting lightly at his waist, sent her breath hissing in through her teeth in shocked reaction.

His jeans were still wet. They weren't actually dripping as they had been on the beach, but the blue cotton was clammy and damp.

Her hand moved up to touch the bare skin of his

chest. It was warmer, but, being this close, she could still scent the tang of the salt that had been left on it, feel it slide under her fingertips.

'I'm sorry,' she whispered and saw the faint frown that drew his black brows together.

'Sorry for what? For this?'

One of his hands touched hers, lightly but still with the effect of pressing her fingers even closer until they were lying flat on his chest. His skin was like oiled silk under her palm, the soft hairs tickling her fingers if they moved.

'Don't apologise for this, *belleza*. Never for this.'

'But you've been so kind—and I…'

A sense of guilt shrivelled the words on her tongue. She had never thanked him properly. He'd rescued her, let her take the first shower while he had been every bit as wet and uncomfortable as she had. And when he'd brought her the towel, he'd held it…

The courtesy of that last gesture overwhelmed her, and, unable to express her gratitude in words, she gave in to the impulse that had been pushing at her brain from the moment he had come close.

Leaning forward, resting both her hands on his shoulders, she lifted her head and pressed what she'd planned as a swift, warm kiss of gratitude on his mouth.

At least that was what she told herself she was doing. And gratitude was all that she would let into her thoughts …

Until her lips actually made contact with the warm softness of his and she felt him first tense, then relax—and respond, kissing her back with a strength and fervour that acted like a match set to bone-dry tinder, setting it blazing in a second. And in the tiny space of time between one heartbeat and the next that kiss brought her body and mind to the point of meltdown from which there was no possible hope of return.

CHAPTER FOUR

SO WHAT the hell happened to restraint?

The question slid into Vito's mind for precisely one second then evaporated straight away in the heat of the sensations he was experiencing.

Restraint had nothing to do with this. It wasn't part of this sort of relationship and it never would be. This wasn't a relationship for waiting, for the future. It was a relationship for taking—for living here and now.

And here and now was where he wanted to be.

Here with this woman's warm, yielding body in his arms. Here, with her soft, giving mouth clamped tight against his, her lips open under his, her tongue dancing with his, with the intimate taste of her blending with his own, creating something totally unique.

Here, where all he had to do was pick her up and carry her to the bed…

In the end he didn't even have to do that. He

simply moved, taking steps backwards away from the bathroom door, and Emily went with him, her mouth still on his, her hands tangled in his hair, clutching at his scalp. Her feet didn't fully touch the ground but she let herself be half walked, half lifted over the green carpet, her body totally supported by his, her eyes closed, her whole being given up to him.

They were at the bed now, with the backs of Emily's legs against the mattress. All it needed was a gentle pressure and her knees bent and she sank down onto the blue covers, her mouth still hot on his, her arms fastened around his neck, pulling him down with her until he was lying on top of her.

'*Emilia—carina, belleza,*' he crooned in his native Italian, the cold, harsh sounds of the English language seeming too rough, too curt for the way he was feeling.

His lips explored her face, felt the softness of her skin beneath them, tasted the subtle flavour that was essentially hers. He kissed her cheek, her chin, caressed his way along the fine line of her jaw, smiling against her face as she moaned low in her throat and angled her head back so that she could have more of his mouth, more of his kisses.

'You like that, hmm?' he murmured and her sigh was all the answer he wanted.

They had no need of words. They communicated so much better this way. The minute that words came into things, the mood changed. If he spoke to her then she rebelled. And, although the spark of mutiny in her eyes had turned him on, the way she'd stood up to him, and that neat little chin firming and coming up defiantly—he dropped another kiss on that particular part of her delightful face—had added an extra *frisson* of interest to the hot attraction he already felt, he much preferred her the way she was now—silent and willing. So willing.

'So let's see what else you like…'

He started what he planned to be a slow voyage of exploration. Starting with her face, he kissed his way over the delicate curve of her ears, her cheekbones, the corners of her closed eyes. And each time his mouth touched she responded with a sigh or a murmur, a sensual twist of her body, a clutch of her fingers in his hair. So that soon the idea of taking anything slow was beyond him. His body was hot and hungry, his need a pulsing ache that made him clench his teeth against the urge to give in to the most basic, most primitive desires that had him in their grip.

His hand slipped between their heated bodies, tugged at the corner of the towel that was folded around her, pulling it loose. The blue material fell away, exposing the soft, pale flesh of her body, the sweet, full curves of her breasts.

It had been too long since he had held a woman in his arms. Too long since he had known the feel of satin-smooth skin, inhaled the intimate perfume of her aroused body. Her blonde hair was like silk across his face, her slender limbs a delicate imprisonment from which he had no wish at all to break free. The warm weight of her breasts fitted perfectly into each hand, the swollen nipples pressing into his palms as he lifted them to his mouth.

'Vito…'

It was more a catch of her breath than a word as he trailed his tongue over the smooth slope of her breast, circling it round and round the pink-flushed tip before drawing it into his mouth and suckling lightly.

Underneath him Emily's slender body moved in restless need, her hips coming up to press against him, driving a groan to escape his control as the movement rubbed the denim of his jeans against the heated sensitivity of his fierce erection.

'More…'

'More, *cara?*'

He turned the question into another form of caress, speaking the words against and around the nipple that his mouth had already teased into further tightness.

'Where would you like more? Here…?'

He let his hands shape those breasts, feeling his own arousal grow even more powerful as he felt them push against him, seeking the pleasure he wanted her to know.

'Or here…?'

Slowly he let one hand trail down, sliding over her ribcage, circling the indentation of her navel, smoothing her hip before he let his fingers drift over the blonde hairs that covered her femininity.

'Everywhere…'

It was a sigh of pleasure, one that made him smile in sensual satisfaction. This was what he had wanted from the second he had first seen her. It was how he had known it would be in the moment that he had held her in his arms, that their lips had touched in that first wild and devastating kiss they had shared out there on the beach.

'Then you shall have "everywhere", *mia cara,*' he promised softly. 'And I…'

'You could have "everywhere" too.' Her tone

was surprisingly petulant. 'If only you'd make it possible.'

The concealing eyelids opened slightly, revealing a reproachful gleam in those soft blue eyes.

'But these...'

One hand tugged at the jeans he still wore.

'Are getting in the way. And besides...'

She compressed her soft mouth in a pretend pout, the wicked glint in her eyes pure provocation. Deliberate provocation, he knew.

'Your jeans are damp! You're rubbing my legs raw.'

'I am? Forgive me, *cara*—forgive me—and help me...'

He lifted himself up, putting his weight on his hands, and knew a thrill like the charge of white-hot electricity run through him as she didn't hesitate but reached immediately for his belt, tugging it open then fumbling with the button at his waist.

But the water that had soaked into the rough denim material had left the fastening too awkward, too stiff for her to manage and eventually he laid his hands over hers, stilling the impatient movement.

'Let me...'

A moment later he kicked away the damp jeans with a sigh of relief, sending his boxer shorts after them before coming back down on the bed beside Emily, pulling her towards him and kissing her hard.

'Now, where had we got to…?' he muttered against her lips.

'Everywhere…' Emily responded, the word slightly muffled by the pressure of his mouth.

'Ah, yes—everywhere.'

This time his hands moved down her back, curving over the neat, tight buttocks, fingers digging into their cushiony softness. And Emily responded in kind, tracing tormentingly arousing patterns over his spine, sliding lower…lower while at the same time her slender body curved against him, breasts crushed against his chest, her pelvis rubbing against his, making his already erect penis harden even more to a point where pleasure almost took on an edge of pain.

She felt so very different from Loretta, whose body had been fuller, skin darker, who—

No! Savagely he slammed a door shut in his mind, closing it against the unwanted thoughts. He didn't want to remember the other woman now. Never wanted to remember her again.

'Vito?' It was a murmur of confusion, a question pushed from her by the way that she had sensed his momentary withdrawal, the fight he had had with himself to rid his mind of unwanted memories.

'*Per niente, tesoro.*'

His reassurance was soft, but distracted because, unwanted as they had been, those memories had stilled his mind, cooled his hunger long enough for him to think a fraction more rationally, remember something that the wild demanding hunger had totally wiped from his mind.

Loretta had tried to con him and he had vowed that he would never, ever be caught that way again.

'Emilia…'

The note of regret in his voice jarred, dropping into the heated atmosphere like cold water splashed onto a glowing fire that was just about to burst into flame.

'Cara—we can't.'

Can't?

If he had slapped her hard in the face he couldn't have shocked her more. Since the moment that he had gathered her up in his arms she had been his. No—face the truth, Emily—she'd been his from that very first kiss and if she'd had any doubts about that they had burned up in the searing heat of the kiss they had shared just now.

She had never felt like this in her life before. *Never.*

Mark had never made her feel this way. Even when they had been close—closer—he had never roused her to such heights with a touch of his hands or his lips, never made her feel that she was burning up inside, aching with need—hurting with it.

So that she felt she might die if he didn't make her his right this moment.

She had wanted this—wanted Vito Corsentino—so much.

And he had wanted her every bit as much, she had been so sure of that.

But now...now he was telling her that they couldn't do this.

'Can't?'

The word was strangled by her disbelief, by the reaction that shot through every nerve in her body. They couldn't stop now. She *couldn't*—already her aroused body was screaming a protest at the way he had stilled, the way his touch had been taken from her.

She was trembling all over, her head spinning until she felt sick.

'What—what do you mean we *can't?*'

Heavy lids hooded the dark eyes, those impossibly long black lashes lying like sooty arcs on his cheeks. But then his gaze lifted, his hands moved up to cup her head, one at each side, and he looked down into her face.

'I have nothing—no protection.'

'Oh, is that all…?'

The words escaped on a rush of relief before she had time to consider how they might sound, the sort of impression they could give.

'I mean—you don't have to worry—I'm on the Pill.'

A pill that she hadn't yet taken today, it was true. A pill that was in her handbag, in her car. But she could fetch it later. She would still take it tonight.

'There won't be any…consequence…from this. I promise.'

Still he looked doubtful. Still he frowned down into her upturned, absorbed face. And just when she had thought she could hope he slowly shook his dark head again.

'A pregnancy is not the only concern…'

It was almost too much. Anger spiked inside her, coming close to making her push him away, push him from her so that she could get off the bed and…

And what?

She had no clothes she could bear to wear. Hers were still in that nasty little damp pile in the corner of the bathroom, so she could hardly adopt a posture of offended dignity and stalk anywhere.

And besides… Looking into his face again, she saw the shadows that clouded his eyes, noted the lines of strain etched around his mouth that revealed the struggle he was having to control himself enough to even make this decision. At least to make it with the rational part of him. His irrational desires were still very much part of the equation if the hot, hard evidence of his arousal that was still pressed against her naked stomach was anything to go by.

He still wanted her and she—oh, she wanted this so much.

It wasn't just the physical hunger that drove her. Deep inside she acknowledged another burning, equally powerful need. The need to assert life in the face of everything that was happening. The need to feel that, for today at least, she was not alone. The need to be held, to be touched, to be *loved*. The need to share with another human being when there had been so much emptiness and pain in her life until now.

And the need to explore the totally unexpected and stunningly powerful connection she had felt to this man from the first moment that he had burst into her life and snatched her up from the waves that were closing over her head.

And so she swallowed the angry reproach, the heated rejection and instead she lifted a hand and touched his lean face very softly, holding those clouded dark eyes with her own as she did so. A heavy lock of jet-black hair had fallen wildly over his forehead and she brushed that back, letting her fingers smooth down over his skull, slide down to the point on his neck where the heavy pulse still beat with an unevenness that betrayed his lack of relaxation. For all that the long, powerful body lay still and apparently acquiescent against her, he was like some streamlined hunting cat, lying waiting and watching, totally alert. Make the wrong move and he would rear up, fling himself away from her and she would never, ever get him back, she had no doubt about that.

And so she spoke as softly, as calmly—as confidently—as she could. Which wasn't easy when her mouth was so dry and her throat threatened to seize up each time she forced a word out of it.

'A pregnancy is not the only concern...' she

echoed in agreement. 'But I can promise you that you have no need to worry over that either. I say again, there will be no consequences of any sort from our—from anything that might happen here between us.'

She tried to make her voice as sure and as confident as she felt inside, but just at the last minute a sudden cold breeze of doubt seemed to brush across her thoughts.

He was tempted. She could see it in his face. It was obvious that he was having every bit as hard a struggle to deny her as she would have to accept if he was going to end this right here and now.

'Vito…'

Still he didn't speak and she could almost hear his brain working, weighing up arguments, debating with himself, coming to no conclusion. But there was some change in his expression, some different light in his eye that gave her hope. And, pushing home what she prayed was an advantage, she lifted her head from the bed and pressed first a gentle, tentative kiss on that sculpted mouth, and then a second, more confident one when he didn't pull away.

He didn't pull away but then he didn't encourage her either, though the hooded lids dropped lower over his eyes to hide their darkness from her.

But under the fingers that rested against his throat his pulse leaped, spiked, then settled into a faster thudding, beat that revealed far more about the way he was feeling than the carefully schooled—into—stone expression on his face.

Gathering her courage, she put her arms up and around his neck, drawing his face down towards hers until their mouths were almost touching. He came willingly enough, with only faint traces of a lingering tension in the muscles of his neck to show any indication of reluctance.

'Vito…' Emily whispered against his cheek. 'Don't fight this. Please don't. There will be no problem, I promise you. Nothing—nothing at all.'

Those dark eyes had closed completely now and under her hands she felt him swallow hard, just once.

'I want this, Vito…I want you…I—'

The words were cut off, what she had been about to say being pushed back down her throat as, with a muttered curse in savage Italian, he abandoned all pretence of fighting. He clamped his mouth down on hers in a fierce, burning kiss that short-circuited every cell in her brain as awareness flooded every other nerve connection, sparking into life again the flames of passion. Flames that she had thought had settled down to just smouldering embers.

How wrong she had been. They hadn't been smouldering but glowing hotly, waiting for someone to throw new fuel onto them so that they could blaze with new vigour, with greater intensity. The need that clawed at her was so sharp, so savage that she gasped aloud as she coped with a hunger that was near to pain.

And it seemed that Vito felt the same way too.

'I can't fight you,' he muttered savagely against her mouth, kissing her again with a force that crushed her lips back against her teeth, his hands twisting in her hair, holding her head so that she was trapped underneath him, unable to move either right or left. She was just where he wanted her, where he could kiss her almost into oblivion.

'I tried to fight myself and that was hard enough—but when you…'

His voice trailed off again as he kissed her more fiercely than before, plundering her mouth, tasting her, invading her.

'I can't deny you.'

'I don't want you to!' Emily managed to gasp as he was forced to lift his head to snatch in some air, allowing her a moment to breathe too. 'What I want is to do this …'

Lifting her head from where it was pillowed on

the duvet, she kissed him again, letting her tongue slide along his lips, teasing his mouth open once again. And in the same moment she let her hands slide over the hard, straight line of his shoulders, down the length of his chest. She tangled her fingertips in the dark hairs, tracing small, teasing circles over the tight male nipples, smiling to herself as she heard his swiftly indrawn breath.

'Emilia…'

It was an ambiguous sound, part warning, part plea for restraint, part encouragement for more.

Emily determined to focus on the encouragement; it fitted much more with the way she was feeling than either of the others. And so she turned her head slightly, let her tongue slide over the bronzed skin, curling round the small nipple that tightened even more under her ministrations.

'You witch!' Vito muttered and her smile grew as she heard in his tone just how close he was to breaking point.

Her actions were having as much effect on her as on him. The taste of his skin, still slightly salty from the sea, tingled on her tongue, and his musky scent acted like a powerful spirit on her senses, intoxicating and liberating her. She kissed his chest, even let her teeth graze lightly over those taut nipples, and all the time she pressed herself against his hard-muscled body while her hands moved over his back, down the long, straight spine, over the tight contours of his buttocks. Her smile grew as she felt him jerk once, tensing under the provocation of her touch.

'You witch!' he said again but in a very different way this time.

Emily let herself meet his eyes for the first time since she had begun this campaign of provocation, and what she saw there wiped the smile from her face, all trace of fun leaving the situation in the space of a single heartbeat. Vito's dark gaze glittered with an almost feverish passion. There was a red line of heat scored across the carved cheekbones and his breath came raw and ragged as he fought for control. Every other thought had left his mind and suddenly all his strength, all his power was concentrated wholly on her and her alone.

Something hard and sharp twisted in Emily's stomach and she really couldn't have said if it was excitement or panic or some mind-blowing combination of the two. The hands that had stroked and teased so confidently faltered, stilled, almost dropped away, then tried to caress him again. Only to be grabbed by Vito and pulled up above her head, brought together on the soft bed-spread, one big hand clamping over the wrists of both of hers to hold her still and imprisoned.

'Oh, no, *carina*,' he muttered, thick and rough. 'You have had your fun and now it's *my* turn. Now I show you the way it can be between us.'

The knot in Emily's stomach tightened, coiling in on itself even more, seeming to send shivers through her lower body, creating an almost electrical shock between her legs where the slow, steady heat that had burned now flared into something wild and fierce. Her body writhed under his, rubbing against the hot, swollen force of his erection, but Vito only laughed deep in his throat and shook his dark head.

'Oh, no, *carissima*, no! If we're going to do this then we're not going to rush things. We're going to take it really slow—and I'm going to show you what it's like to really *want*, to really hunger. By the time I've finished you'll be so hungry for me that you'll be screaming…'

She was screaming now, inside at least, Emily thought, but she couldn't let him know that. She also didn't dare to wonder how he could make things any more sensuous, how he could arouse her any further, how…

Her thoughts stopped dead as Vito lowered his mouth to hers, taking her lips in a slow, sensual caress that was so very different from the fierce assault of just moments before. His mouth seduced hers, his tongue teased its way inside, his breath mingled with hers, and the taste of him was far richer, more satisfying than the finest meal she had ever enjoyed.

And he took his time over everything.

He kissed her until her head swam. He left her breathless and yearning and hungry for more. Because somehow he seemed to sense when she had almost—almost—had enough and then he moved on. His tormenting, tantalising, seductive mouth left hers and kissed its way over her chin, along her jaw and down, down her neck.

And still his hand kept her prisoner. Still he held her while she writhed underneath him, longing— needing—to touch in response and being so totally controlled that she was unable to. There was no harshness in his restraint, no cruelty in his hold, only a firm, cool grip that she couldn't fight against even if she tried.

By the time that his dark head and that teasing, exciting mouth had slipped ever lower, covering the path of soft skin to the slope of her left breast, she was incapable of doing anything other than surrender. Her senses were so roused, the need that burned through her white-hot in intensity, so that when he used his free hand to lift her breast to his mouth, taking the distended nipple into its heat and suckling softly, she was almost swooning in delight. And as soon as the smallest moan of pleasure escaped her he increased the pressure of his mouth on her, stimulating and enticing until every nerve that radiated from her nipple was stinging with a pleasure that was so intense it was close to pain.

'Vito!' she cried but his only response was a rich, dark chuckle low in his throat as, still keeping his mouth on her breast, he moved his hand lower, let it slide between her legs, wicked fingers knowing exactly where to find and precisely how to touch the other tight, hungry nub that yearned for his attention.

'Oh—Vito…'

His name was the only word her tongue was capable of forming, the only thought in her head. She was lost, abandoned, adrift on a golden tide of pleasure that picked her up and carried her away, closing over her head with every bit of the force that the cold sea waves had turned on her earlier that day.

But now there wasn't an inch of her that was cold. Instead, every inch, every nerve, every cell was ablaze with burning hunger. And the heat built and built as Vito kept up his sensual assault on her body, until her head thrashed from side to side on the denim-blue duvet, her hands straining to be freed from his powerful imprisonment.

But it was only when he finally pushed her legs apart and eased himself between them that he actually let her go. And then she was too far gone into a world of scorching sensation that she barely noticed he had freed her. Instead every part of her mind was now focused on the core of her body, on the spot where the heated head of his erection was pushing at her, stretching her, driving into her with a force and strength that made her breath escape in a wild gasp of shocked delight.

'Emilia…'

'Vito…'

Her name and his were spoken together, blending into one wild, hungry cry of fierce excitement that echoed through the silence of the room. And as Emily belatedly realised that her hands were free her only thought was to fling her arms around the neck of the man above her, close her hands over the strength of his shoulders. She felt the hard muscles bunch as they tensed and relaxed and then tensed again with each forceful thrust into her hungry body, fingers digging into his skin as he took her higher, harder, faster, until she was spinning out of control, out of the world, out of her body. She knew that Vito was there, but Vito was all she knew. And all she wanted to know. He was the only real thing in a world that had hazed into insignificance. The only solid strength where everything else had melted away, out of her sight and out of her grasp.

She was reaching for something else. Something brighter and fiercer and far, far stronger than she had ever known before. And somewhere, barely registered, almost hidden at the back of her mind, was the stunning, unbelievable realisation that this was something they were heading towards *together.* That this was amazing, special, unique because it was shared, because Vito was making sure that she was right there with him, all the way.

And that thought was so astounding that it was the one that finally took her over the edge and into a golden, glowing, mind-shattering oblivion.

CHAPTER FIVE

THE sun was warm on the top of Vito's head as he strolled along the promenade towards where Emily had parked her car the previous day. Out in the bay the sea lapped against the shore in a lazy, placid way that made it seem almost impossible that it had ever been as wild and dangerous as it had yesterday afternoon.

This sea, calm and almost unmoving in the sunlight, would never have caused the problems it had yesterday. It would never have been the danger it had been for Emily, never have knocked her off her feet, almost drowned her.

So he had to be grateful that it was like this today and not yesterday—or that it was yesterday that Emily had decided to go for the paddle in the sea that had resulted in the accident that had brought her into his life.

Into his life...

Vito paused for a moment, a smile curving the

corners of his mouth, eyes narrowed against the sun as he stared out at the far horizon, idly tossing the key he held up and then catching it in one hand as he remembered the scene he had woken to in his flat that morning.

He had no idea at what time he had fallen asleep. Only knew that it had been a long time after Emily had finally succumbed to the exhaustion that their long hours of passionate lovemaking had produced in her. But he had stayed awake for much longer, lying beside her, propped up on one elbow, simply watching her sleep. He had stared down into her relaxed and peaceful face, listening to her soft breathing, watching the way her eyelids flickered occasionally.

He had lost count of how many times they had made love altogether. That first passionate coming together had only been the start of it. After that they had spent the rest of the evening in bed, only pausing perhaps for an hour or so when hunger and thirst had forced them into the kitchen in search of the coffee he had planned to make some time before. Eventually satiated and content, he had fallen asleep like her, only to be woken as the dawn light flooded into the room by the feel of her soft hands exploring his body, the caress of kisses on his skin.

And it had all begun again.

But now, at last, they had decided that they had better start the day. And that meant that they had had to consider facing the world again. Much as they both might have wanted to stay holed up in the flat forever, they had to consider reality—at least just a little bit.

And that was when the mood had changed.

Just as it had been yesterday when he had stopped kissing her and given her the freedom to speak, so now this morning, when they had finally got out of bed, Emily had suddenly seemed to become someone else. She was edgy, twitchy, and her mind had definitely been elsewhere. When he had got up to make more coffee, she had hurried into the bathroom, only to emerge a few moments later with a bundle of something in her hands and a horrified expression on her face.

'Look at this! Look at this mess!'

She shook out the crumpled items that then revealed themselves to be the T-shirt and jeans she had worn the day before. Having spent the night on the floor in the bathroom they were creased beyond repair and obviously still unpleasantly wet and cold.

'That's what happens if you throw soaking-wet

clothes in a corner and leave them there over-night.'

Vito shrugged his lack of concern.

'My T-shirt's much the same after a night in the washer—and my jeans...'

He waved a hand towards the open door into the bedroom, where the jeans he had discarded the night before were visible still on the floor beside the bed.

'They might be OK to wear after being washed and ironed...'

'But what am I going to wear until then?'

It was a wail of despair, one that grated uncom-fortably after the sensually leisurely lovemaking that had started their day, making him frown his disapproval.

'Does it matter?'

'Of course it matters!'

She really looked badly upset—over a few clothes?

'It doesn't to me.'

He turned a warmly appreciative glance on her naked body. OK, so much of it was currently con-cealed behind the bundle of clothing she held, but he had had plenty of experience of just what the hidden bits were like, enough to give him some very pleasant memories.

'I'm perfectly happy for you to stay that way all day,' he drawled lazily.

The remark earned him an unexpected flashing glare of reproof.

'You might be, but I'm not! I can't just provide a floor show for you all day.'

'You certainly are not at your best in the mornings, are you?'

With an effort Vito reined in the flare of temper that her unjust retort threatened to spark off.

'Have you got out of the wrong side of the bed perhaps? That was not what I meant to say and you know it!'

'I'm sorry!'

She obviously made an effort to shake herself out of the irritated mood that had suddenly descended from nowhere.

'But I do need something to wear.'

'Well, that's no problem. I got something out for you last night before we—got distracted. I left them on the chair by the bed.'

The kettle boiled as he spoke and he turned to switch it off, pour the hot water on top of the coffee grounds in the waiting cafetière.

Then he realised that Emily was standing beside him again and from the silence, something in the atmosphere, he knew that she still wasn't content. Turning, he saw that the expression on her face confirmed as much.

'Is this what you meant?'

A wave of her hand indicated the navy T-shirt and boxer shorts that she had pulled on in double-quick time. When he nodded yes she frowned and shook her head.

'What is it now?' he sighed. If the truth was told, he thought the outfit rather appealing. The T-shirt hung loose on her slender frame but the soft material clung to the swell of her breasts, the curves of her hips, and the boxers revealed a welcome amount of the long, slender legs that had so recently been tangled up with his in the most satisfyingly intimate way. The clothes were perfectly adequate for drinking coffee in.

After that he looked forward to peeling them off her again and taking her back to bed.

'You look fine to me.'

'But I can't go out like this!'

Out? That was unexpected and not at all welcome. Neither was the thought that she might, after all, be planning to leave.

'Why would you want to go out?'

'Vito, all my stuff—my handbag, my phone—

it's all in my car. And my car is over five minutes' walk away down a public road. I can hardly go out there like this.'

Once more she looked down at the clothes she was wearing, her mouth twisting wryly.

So that was what was on her mind. The rush of relief at the thought that she wasn't actually planning on leaving made his head spin. He hadn't realised until now just how much he had relied on this not actually being a one-night stand. He didn't do one-night stands and one night was definitely not long enough to grow tired of this particular woman.

'Is that all? *Non c'e problema!* Just give me a moment and I'll get some clothes on. Then I will go to your car and collect anything you want. You can start making breakfast while I'm gone.'

Was she going to refuse? Just for a moment it had looked as if she would but then she obviously accepted that she had no other choice.

'OK,' she nodded, though the smile she had given him flashed on and off with all the speed of a neon sign, and about as much warmth.

But out here in the brightness of the day, with the sea glinting in the sun and the prospect of the rest of the weekend ahead of them, none of that seemed to matter any more. Vito turned from his contemplation of the horizon and headed down the promenade towards where Emily's small blue car was parked, the smile coming back to his mouth as he did so.

In spite of her protestations of yesterday, she had stayed the night—and what a night—and she was still here for breakfast. He was damn sure he could make her stay for the rest of the weekend and in that time he would get her number, her address and—

He stopped dead in amazement as realisation suddenly struck him.

He still didn't even know her surname. Emily was all she had ever said. Emily what? He would ask her first thing, as soon as he got back to the flat.

And then he supposed that would mean that he'd have to explain the truth about himself too. It was a pity, as he'd enjoyed the freedom her not knowing had given him. He'd not had to wonder whether she was with him for himself or was the same sort of gold-digger Loretta had turned out to be.

He was at the car now, bending to unlock the driver's door. Emily had said that she'd pushed her handbag under the front passenger seat for safety and he could just see the thin black strap from here. Leaning forward, he caught hold of it, tugged, pulling it towards him.

'*Dannazione!*'

It was open, the narrow zip on the top unfastened, and the jerky movement had made several small items fall out. The comb and the lipstick case were easy to reach but he had to scrabble a bit to get hold of the phone. He was about to toss it into the bag with the other things when he noticed that it had been left switched on all night. He still had it in his hand when suddenly it started to ring. Automatically he thumbed it on.

'*Ciao?*'

There was a stunned silence at the other end of the line then a bemused and suspicious female voice said, 'Who the hell is that? I thought this was Emily's number.'

'Oh, *scusi,*' Vito hastened to apologise. 'It is Emily's phone. But I'm afraid that she is not here right now. Can I take a message for her?'

The woman he was speaking to hesitated then sighed impatiently.

'I suppose it will have to do. But can you make sure she gets this? It's important.'

'I'll tell her as soon as I see her,' Vito assured

her and then listened intently to what the woman had to say.

It changed his mood completely,

His hand tightened on the small silver-coloured phone and he straightened up slowly, still listening. From this position he could see his own face reflected in the car's wing mirror and as he watched he saw how his expression changed. Watched every last trace of the smile that had lingered on his mouth fade, leaving it stiff and tight and drawn into a hard, thin line. Watched the cold darkness enter his eyes and turn them into shards of black ice. He kept totally silent until the message was completed and then, when the unknown woman said, 'You will tell her, won't you?' he nodded his head firmly even though he knew she couldn't see him.

'Oh, yes,' he said with freezing cold emphasis. 'Yes, I'll tell her. Don't worry, I'll make sure she gets the message, you need have no doubt about that.'

And as he snapped off the phone and headed back along the promenade towards the flat his expression was dark and grim—as dark and grim as the mood that had suddenly descended.

He'd tell Emily all right—oh, yes, he'd make very, very sure that she got the message. And he was going to get a great deal of pleasure out of watching the way her face—her cheating, lying, beautiful face—changed as she realised that he now knew the real truth about her.

Emily pulled her jeans out of the tumble-drier and shook them hard, frowning as she did so. The movement smoothed them out a bit, but not much. They still looked terrible. And they were still very damp.

Perhaps if she ironed them…

If Vito possessed an iron, of course. She had hunted round the small kitchen but hadn't been able to find one. She'd have to ask him when he got back.

When he got back.

How long did it take to walk a few hundred yards and grab a handbag?

Tossing the jeans back into the drier for now— she could wear them creased if she had to, and she would probably have to—Emily paced back and forth across the kitchen floor, clenching and un-clenching her fists at her sides.

She needed that bag—needed the phone that was in it. Ruth had promised that she would ring at ten-thirty and it was after quarter-past now. And Ruth was *never* late. In fact, if she had a fault it was that she was often too early, so putting people out by appearing or ringing before they were ready. But at least she'd switched off the phone before going onto the beach yesterday, so if Ruth did ring early then…

Emily paused, pushing her hand through her hair as she frowned thoughtfully.

She had switched it off, hadn't she? She was sure she had.

The sound of a key in the door pushed her into action.

Make breakfast, Vito had said, and she didn't want it to look as if she had spent the whole time he'd been out simply pacing up and down, even if she had. She had had no chance at all to explain the situation to him and she had no idea how he was going to react. She had a lot of explaining to do. She hadn't even got as far as giving him her full name last night—they hadn't exactly spent much time on introductions!

Feeling red heat flare up over her face, she hurriedly swung away from the door, grabbing the cafetière of coffee that Vito had made before he'd gone out—coffee she hadn't even touched—and dumping the contents in the sink, turning the tap with unnecessary force to swill it all away. Behind her she heard the door open, felt the faint rush of air, and knew that Vito had arrived.

'Sorry about breakfast—I…got distracted.'

She sounded far too airy and careless, unbelievably so. In her own ears it was obvious that she was covering something up and she nerved herself for the inevitable question about what was going on.

To her surprise it didn't come. Instead the silence behind her was so deep, so total, that for a moment she wondered if Vito had in fact appeared or if she had got it wrong and he'd not actually come into the kitchen yet.

But a quick glance over her shoulder told her that he was there, in the doorway, one broad shoulder resting against the doorframe and his arms folded across his chest.

'Do you want coffee now?'

'OK.'

It was curt, abrupt. So abrupt that it had her swinging round to face him. And immediately a feeling of unease made a sensation like the flutter of hundreds of butterfly wings start up in the pit of her stomach.

This wasn't the same man who had set out to fetch her handbag just ten minutes or so before. Then he had been easy-going, calm, even smiling. Now he was a withdrawn, cold-eyed stranger. That stance, with the long, powerful body leaning against the door, might look relaxed but she could see a stiffness about the way he held himself that told a very different story. Those arms were folded just a little *too* tightly and the sexy mouth was clamped shut, his jaw clenched, as if he was holding back something ominous.

'Is something wrong?'

Vito returned her scrutiny with a level stare, one that held no warmth, not even a light in the deep grey eyes.

'Why? Is there anything you're expecting to go wrong?

'N-no, but—did you get my handbag?'

The feeling of uncertainty made her voice jump unevenly. Perhaps he hadn't been able to find her bag and that was what the problem was. Had someone broken into her car—taken her things from it? Or perhaps they had stolen the car itself.

But then Vito unfolded his arms and picked up the black leather handbag that had been lying on the floor at his feet, lifting it so that it dangled in his grip, looking absurdly small against the size of the hand that held it.

'Oh, great!'

She'd grabbed at it before she thought that she was giving herself away. The zip was partially open and she only had to push it back a little way to check that the phone was there and—yes—it was switched off. She'd have to switch it back on again soon if…

'Everything's still there.' Vito's voice intruded into her thoughts. At least, she knew it was Vito's voice. It came from where he was standing and she saw his lips move. But it wasn't the voice she remembered. It wasn't the voice of the man that she had met yesterday, the stunning, sexy Sicilian who had rescued her and then charmed her into his bed. And it wasn't the voice that had whispered to her in the night, that had enticed her to stay, told her she was beautiful, and finally had called out her name as he lost himself in the moment of ecstasy.

This voice was cold, like his eyes; cold and dangerous.

'Of course it is.'

She tried a smile but saw no answering lightness in his face, no change in that dark, blank stare.

'Thank you!'

Another smile, and again no reaction. On an impulse she moved forward, pressed a kiss against his mouth. Surely *that* would lighten his mood. Surely he would respond…

But Vito didn't. Instead her lips came up against the hard, unyielding tightness of his mouth, almost bruising her against the force of his rejection so that she put up her hand to cover her lips, trying to soothe the unexpected hurt.

'Vito…'

'*Emilia…*' It was a cynical, dark-toned echoing of her own voice, no trace of warmth or friendliness in the sound. 'Don't you think you have something you should be telling me?'

'I do?'

Vito just nodded his dark head slowly, keeping his eyes fixed on the pallor of her face. It was as if in the time that he had been outside, the man she had known as Vito had been taken out of his body and a new and totally different personality had been implanted in it.

She didn't know what he wanted and the clock on the kitchen wall was slowly ticking away the fifteen minutes she'd had before the phone call was due. There were only five of them left now and…

And then it dawned on her.

Of course. The handbag. She had asked him to fetch her bag and it had all her personal things in it—her purse, her credit cards, her driver's licence, all in the name of…

'I never introduced myself properly last night.'

'No, you didn't.'

There was a strange emphasis on the words, a dark and worrying one. She might even have said there was an edge of menace in it but that sounded fanciful and over-dramatic. Probably she was just so badly on edge that she had put too much into the sound.

'You—you gave me your full name and I never actually got around to telling you mine.'

She glanced at him as the words died away, looking for some response or at least an inclination of his head, a nod, anything to indicate that he had heard. That he was listening to her and was open to what she was saying.

But there was nothing. Just that same dark, opaque-eyed stare that reminded her of the eyes in a carved marble statue, blank and unrevealing, in a way that dried her mouth in apprehension to see it.

'I—I'm Emily Lawton.'

Foolishly—ridiculously—*impossibly* after all that had passed between them in the night, she held out her hand to him as if it were the first time they had met. Vito's dark eyes followed the gesture and one corner of his mouth quirked up in what might have been a smile. But when his eyes met Emily's once again, the hard black depths she looked into told her that there had been no warmth in the reaction at all. Instead it was a brutally cynical response, dismissing her attempt at contact.

'So you're Emily Lawton,' he said at last, and the contempt in his voice seemed to sear over her skin, scouring off a much needed protective layer, leaving her feeling raw and exposed. 'Well, I wish I could say that it was nice to meet you but I'm afraid that would be a lie.'

'What?'

She couldn't believe what she was hearing—or the hateful, goading way it was spoken.

'It would be a lie because that isn't really your name, is it?'

'It isn't…?'

She couldn't find the strength of mind to follow what he was saying. It didn't make any sense. He was talking in riddles.

What had happened? Dear God, what *could* have happened in the ten minutes or so that he had been outside to turn him from the ardent, passionate lover of the night into the iceman of today?

'Vito—please! I don't understand.'

She couldn't help herself, her hand came out, caught hold of his, curled her fingers around it.

Surely the touch would break through whatever wall of anger and withdrawal had surrounded him so that she could reach him, speak to him, communicate with him at least. Surely he hadn't forgotten about last night and the stunning fires of passion they had lit between them?

But it seemed that he had. Forgotten or dismissed them totally from his thoughts, because he shook her hand off roughly, pulling away from it with an expression of such disgust that it seemed that he believed her touch might actually contaminate him. He hadn't moved from his position in the doorway but it seemed to her that his long body had stiffened even more, held firmly away from her so that he appeared more distant than ever.

And she couldn't find a way to reach him.

'Vito, what is it? What's happened?'

'I believe the English expression is, you tell me.'

'But I've nothing to tell.'

'No?'

Sharp as a bullet and, from the way that she felt the impact of his scorn, almost as deadly.

'Are you sure?'

'Vito, will you please explain—?'

'Explain?'

The harsh crack of laughter was so rough, so brutal that she brought her head up in shock, staring at him in disbelief and confusion.

'I believe that you are the one who owes me the explanation.'

'I do? But…'

In the whirling haze that was her mind she couldn't find anything that she thought she had done wrong. Anything that she needed to explain to him. He had been the one who had insisted that she came back here. He had suggested that she stayed. He had…

The click of the big hand on the clock moving forward warned her that time was passing. Any minute now and Ruth would be ringing. She couldn't afford to miss this call.

'I'm sorry, Vito, but I don't understand—and I don't have the time to talk about this right now…

Her hand was inside her bag, finding the phone, pulling it out.

'And I have to take a call…'

'No, you don't.'

He moved then, straightening up and coming to still her hand on the bag, and just the few inches of adjustment seemed to make him even taller than ever, towering over her in a way that made a shiver of apprehension run coldly down the length of her spine.

'Vito—I do! I do…' she tried again but the words died on her tongue as he shook his dark head in adamant refusal. And it was as she looked into his hard, implacable face that the first faint hints of suspicion began to dawn and with them came the cold, creeping fingers of fear of what might have happened.

But how could it have happened?

'You don't need to take the call,' he repeated with cruel emphasis, 'because I already did. I spoke to—Ruth, I believe her name is.'

Emily actually felt all the blood drain from her face. She felt her skin grow cold and clammy in the same moment that her head spun in shock.

It couldn't be true. He couldn't be saying what she thought he was.

'No.'

She shook her head despairingly, knowing there was no hope when he reached out and caught hold of her chin, stilling the movement roughly. Hard fingers dug into her skin, making her wince as he forced her to meet the black intensity of his eyes that seemed to burn right into her skull with the power of a terrible laser.

'Yes,' he said, coldly emphatic. 'Oh, yes, Emily, *mia belleza…*'

His tone laced the terms of endearment with bitter poison that turned them into the exact opposite of their literal meaning.

'Yes, I spoke to her, and what she told me means that I now know your real name. Your *full* name.'

'My full—but I told you—Emily—'

The violent gesture he made, bringing down his free hand in a savage, slashing moment, cut off what she had been about to say and she could only freeze, staring up at him in shock and horror as he spoke again.

'Your *full* name, *mia cara,*' he muttered savagely, flinging the words into her face like blows. 'Because it's not just Emily Lawton, is it? It's *Mrs* Emily Lawton. You're married!'

CHAPTER SIX

'YOU'RE married!'

The words had tasted so vile on his tongue that once they were out in the open Vito wished that he could pour himself a glass of water and swill out his mouth, washing away the foul taste.

But Emily—*Mrs Emily Lawton*—was between him and the sink and to reach it he would have to move past her, which, in the confined space of the tiny kitchen, would mean that he would inevitably have to brush up against her. And right now he felt he would rather die than do that.

But what mistake could there be? She was married, damn it. *Married.*

'I never *lied.* The question wasn't asked. You talk about honour!' she spluttered. '*You* answered my phone—listened to a personal call. I wouldn't describe invading my privacy like that as something *honourable.*'

'*Perdon?*'

So was there any hope that Vito might be different? That he might give her a chance to explain that the situation was not really what it seemed? It certainly didn't look like it. He was too savagely angry to listen to reason. His face was set so hard that it might have been carved from granite, the beautiful mouth compressed into just a thin, cruel line. His eyes seared over her in an expression of such total contempt that she was frankly surprised that she hadn't shrivelled into a pile of nothing but dust under the impact of his burning scorn. And the contrast between the way it was now and the way it had been last night clawed at her already raw heart, tearing it to pieces inside her.

'And all *I* remember is that you were not exactly reluctant.'

Emily shook her head hard so that her blonde hair flew wildly into her face, covering it for the couple of seconds it took her to collect herself, swallow down the tears that stung cruelly at the backs of her eyes. She wouldn't let them fall. *Couldn't* let them. She would rather die than let him see how much he had hurt her, the way that his words had slashed wounds on top of wounds that he'd already created.

Walking back to his flat with his mind spinning from the impact of that appalling phone call, Vito had found it impossible to think straight about anything. His memory had kept throwing up flashes of scenes from the previous night, scenes in which Emily was kissing him, touching him. Scenes where she was in his arms, in his bed, with her gloriously sexy body underneath him, opening to him—scenes he could now no longer remember without the terrible sense of betrayal and disgust that ripped through him as he recalled them.

And the one thing he had been sure of then, with no room for any possible doubt in his mind, had been the fact that he would never, ever want to touch Emily Lawton again. If he did, he felt that it would actually make him feel as if he could retch out his soul, so dark and deep was the disgust he felt for what she had done.

But now, with just his hand on her chin, holding her face, her beautiful, lying, cheating face towards his, he could still feel the stinging sense of intense physical awareness race through him, no matter how much he wanted to deny it. His mind might be telling him one thing but every one of his senses was screaming something very different at him. Just the small contact with one hand was bad enough, but if he had to brush past her, his body making contact with hers, then the memories of the night they had shared might just make him go up in flames all over again.

So why didn't she say something in response to his accusation?

Because she couldn't. It was written all over her face. It was there in those stunning eyes. It was even, he was convinced, hardening the soft rose-pink temptation of her mouth. The mouth he had kissed so often and so passionately last night while all the time she had been lying…

'You're married!'

'Yes.'

Stark and simple, and flatly emotionless, it was the last thing he wanted to hear. Which was something that shocked him right to the core of his being. Was it possible that even now, even after all that he had heard from this Ruth in the phone call that had held him frozen as he listened to it, he had still hoped that she might say something else? Had he truly hoped that she might deny the accusation, declare it was all false—or that there had been some terrible mistake?

Realising that he still held her chin, he released her abruptly, snatching back his hand as if he had foolishly plunged it right into the heart of a blazing fire. That was very much the way he felt mentally too. Badly burned by her deceit.

It was only when he saw the way her head moved that he realised how in the same instant that he had released her she had pulled away too, so that their combined actions had an almost violent impact. One that had her taking a couple of involuntary steps backwards and away from him before she caught herself and regained her balance. But in that instant it was as if the small gap of flooring between them had opened up into a wide, dangerous chasm. One that would be impossible to bridge at any point now or in the future.

Which was just how he wanted it. He'd been lied to by one woman; he wasn't about to let it happen again.

'You admit it?' he demanded, voice harsh and rough as his feelings. 'You admit that you lied?'

But that brought her head up again sharply. Standing straight and tall, she turned wide, defiant eyes on his face, the fury that sparked in them making him feel as if electricity was actually fizzing through her and that if he had still been touching her he would have felt the shock of it running along his own nerves.

'But you didn't think it might be...honourable...to mention it?'

'Honour!'

The blue eyes opened even wider and the look she turned on him was a clever approximation to outraged virtue. So clever that it almost convinced.

Almost.

They said attack was the best form of defence, but Emily wasn't at all sure that that really was the wisest move in this case. From the black scowl on Vito's face, she was sure she was only stirring up more trouble for herself. But she wasn't going to stand by and let Vito savage her when he didn't know the truth.

No one knew the truth about her so-called marriage. Except for herself and Mark—and now only herself.

At least he had the grace to look shamefaced at the accusation.

'I apologise for that,' he returned stiffly, so stiffly that Emily rolled her eyes in exasperation and disbelief.

'Oh, at least make it sound as if you mean it!'

That earned her another savage glare from those molten black eyes.

'I do mean it!' he snapped, icy precision in every word, even the beautiful accent erased by the cold notes of fury that made his voice strangely crisp and curt. 'I should not have listened to your phone message. But you are not going to claim that two wrongs make something right?'

'No, of course I'm not going to claim that! But it isn't how you think.'

Emily made a move towards him, instinctively reaching out a hand to touch his arm, hoping that the contact might just make him pause, make him listen. But the flashing glare he turned on her made her snatch back the foolish gesture before her fingers had even made contact with his arm.

'Oh, is it not? And are you now going to say that I should doubt the evidence of my own ears?'

'No …' It was low, miserable, but there was nothing else she could say.

'I know what I heard. Or are you saying that your friend Ruth—?'

'She's my sister-in-law. And no friend of mine.'

'Ah, so she is the one who lied when she said that you have a husband?'

'No…' It was even lower. Even more miserable.

Vito angled his head to one side, being deliberately provocative, Emily was sure.

'What did you say? I could not hear you.'

Oh, I just bet you couldn't, Emily muttered in

the privacy of her thoughts. But she didn't dare provoke him quite that much. She was suddenly painfully aware of the fact that she was standing here, in his kitchen, with his big, strong body between her and the door, and common sense or self-preservation at least dictated that she should not make any foolishly risky moves.

'I said no, she didn't lie about that.'

'I thought not. She was determined that I should listen to what she had to say. She was adamant about it.'

'Of course she was.'

Ruth had never liked her, even from the start of her ill-fated marriage. Ruth would never hear a word said against Mark and so she had hidden from the truth about the man her brother was. No one had believed Emily's claims. Mark had been too good at pretending in public for that.

No, he had set himself against her just like everyone else. She would probably never convince him, but that didn't mean she had to take everything he threw at her without fighting back.

'None of this seemed to matter to you last night!' she flung at him, the pain of remembering the beauty of the night, of the passion they had shared, making her voice break in bitterness. 'I don't recall you asking me if I was married or even showing any interest in it.'

'I believed I didn't need to.'

He grabbed at her left hand, held it up in front of her eyes, deliberately lifting the ring finger up to isolate it.

The empty ring finger. She'd taken off her ring months ago, when she had believed that the ending of her marriage was simply a formality.

'You weren't wearing a ring.'

'But you didn't check…'

'Oh, so now I'm the one who should have said something?'

'Well, if it mattered so much to you, yes!'

Emily snatched back her hand, cradling it against her as if it had been burned.

'All I remember is that you were determined to get me into your bed, no matter what.'

Vito's tone was low and deadly, striking at her like a cruel blade.

'I gave you what you wanted.'

'No…'

In the darkness at the back of her mind she said goodbye to the tiny unformed hopes and dreams that only now was she admitting to herself had begun to seed in her thoughts. Hopes of something more; hopes of a future. Hopes of sharing something with this man that she had never known with anyone else before.

Hopes that she had been a fool even to let slip into her mind. She wasn't even going to let herself consider the effect on her heart.

'No you didn't! You took what you wanted and gave me what you thought I wanted! Those things just aren't the same.'

'You wanted me.'

'I tried to get away from you, if you remember rightly. I fought against coming here—refused to do so.'

'But only to add spice to things,' Vito returned with such supreme arrogance that it literally took her breath away, leaving her gasping in incredulity. 'You pretended you needed persuading— I went along with the game. It's part of the way these things are played.'

'Game...played...'

Emily couldn't believe what she was hearing. Her head was spinning as if the words he'd tossed into her stunned face had actually been cruel blows, slaps that had knocked her physically off balance. Putting out a hand, she grabbed hold of the back of a nearby chair, clenching her fingers tight over it until the knuckles showed white under her skin.

'I wasn't playing at anything!'

'Of course you were.'

Vito dismissed her protest with total scorn.

'You weren't honest enough to admit that you wanted me from the start so you manipulated the situation so that I would have to persuade you.'

'You were walking away from me!'

'Only because I knew you would call me back. And you did, didn't you? You barely let me get halfway up the beach before you were calling after me.'

'And I suppose I started the storm as well.'

The look he slanted her from those dark, brilliant eyes said without words that if he could believe she had the power to do just that, then he would accuse her of it. Emily didn't know whether the sensations bubbling up inside her, pushing their way into her throat, were the need to laugh slightly hysterically at his effrontery or to scream out loud. And she frankly despaired of the way that even in this nightmare of a situation her crazy, out-of-control senses could still spark at the sound of his voice, the gleam of light on his skin, the way that those lush black lashes lay against his cheek.

'You were lucky there. It saved you from actually having to admit that you wanted to stay.'

This time the shock of his interpretation was so great that Emily actually sank down into the chair, her legs refusing to support her any more.

'You arrogant pig!' she gasped. 'You're just interpreting everything so that it fits the twisted way you want to believe things happened.'

'As opposed to you, who simply didn't bother to tell some inconvenient truths that might have got in the way of you getting what you wanted,' Vito flung back. 'What worries me is just how many other things you might have lied to me about.'

Behind Vito, the tumble-drier suddenly rumbled to a halt so that his coldly angry words fell into a sudden silence that was almost shocking after the way the machine had kept up a constant, rather ominously growling accompaniment to the angry, bitter words they had been flinging at each other, like distant thunder muttering and threatening on the horizon.

'What…'

Emily could only stare at him in disbelief and confusion, unable to imagine what he meant. But then a slow, shivering sense of suspicion crept over her skin and she forced herself to her feet, feeling far too vulnerable sitting down while he loomed over her with his face as dark as any of the storm clouds that had filled the skies yesterday.

'You said you were on the Pill, for one.'

'I am on the Pill!'

Emily looked round frantically, hunting for her handbag so that she could find the packet of pills and throw them in his face. But then something in his tone, in his eyes, brought her to an abrupt halt as the truth of what he was saying dawned.

Last night she'd let this pass. She'd been too crazy for this man, too caught up in the passion he had created in her to think straight, and so she'd let him get away with it. But not this time.

'Why, you…!'

Blind anger launched her straight at him, her hand swinging up and aiming for his cheek, the need to wipe that cold-eyed sneer from his face wiping out any consideration of the wisdom or otherwise of such an action.

Whether she would actually have slapped him or not, she didn't know—and she didn't get a chance to find out. Vito had seen the change in her expression and interpreted it perfectly. His reactions were lightning-swift too as he reached out and caught her hand in mid-air, clamping hard fingers tightly round her wrist.

'Oh, no, you don't,' he warned but Emily was beyond listening to the note of danger in his words.

'Aren't you afraid of touching me?' she challenged, her blue-eyed gaze clashing sharply with his black. 'I mean—you never know if you might catch something nasty from me after all!'

Worryingly Vito's punishing grip tightened and she held her breath in apprehension. But sheer stubbornness kept her from looking away, determination making her face out his black-eyed glare.

For a moment her stomach tied itself in tight, twisting knots as she waited to see which way he jumped, then she felt her hand dropped so abruptly that the movement yanked roughly at her shoulder.

'I already have,' Vito muttered. 'I've caught a nasty dose of self-disgust which has left me with a foul taste in my mouth and an urgent need to have a very long and very hot shower.'

He was already turning towards the door as he spoke but he paused to glance back over his shoulder. Emily wouldn't have thought it possible for his eyes to get any darker, his expression any colder, but the look he gave her seemed to turn every trace of blood in her veins into ice, freezing her heart into total stillness.

'I would prefer it if you weren't here when I'm finished.'

CHAPTER SEVEN

SHE supposed she should have expected it but it still rocked the ground beneath her feet, making her feel as unsteady and nauseous as if she had actually been on board a ship in a very rough sea.

'You're throwing me out?'

That brought him swinging back round to face her and the slowness with which he moved, the contemptuous survey that he subjected her to, obsidian eyes sliding over her from the top of her head to the spot where her bare toes curled in pained embarrassment on the floor, made her wish she were invisible. That or somewhere else entirely.

She was suddenly painfully aware of the way she was dressed, something that shock and distress had wiped from her mind. So now the recollection that she was wearing Vito's T-shirt and Vito's boxer shorts made her skin flame with colour, her cheeks burning painfully hot.

'You surely didn't think I was going to let you

stay? In case you haven't got the message, *signora*....'

The pointed emphasis on the married form of the word made Emily wince miserably but if Vito noticed then he gave no sign of having done so.

'I do not sleep with other men's wives. I never have and I never would—not willingly. It goes against everything I believe to be right. You may be able to forget your marriage vows but believe me, my conscience is not as jaded as yours appears to be.'

'You don't understand…'

She had to try once more in spite of the fact that she knew he wasn't going to give her the chance to explain.

And she was right. Vito's hand came down in a savage, slashing movement as he cut off her stumbling attempt to put her case.

'On the contrary, I do understand—and I don't like it one little bit. You've grown tired of your wedding vows and decided to play the field—but not with me, *belleza,* not with me. And if I'd known that yesterday then I wouldn't have touched you. As it is, I still feel dirty just to think of it. So I'm going to have that shower and you…'

He marched towards the door, held it wide open.

'You can get your things and get out. Don't trouble to leave the clothes you have on, I'd only burn them. Quite frankly, I wouldn't want to touch them after they've been on your unfaithful, immoral body. And I don't want you around here any longer than you have to be. The sooner you're out of here and out of my sight, the happier I'll be.'

There was no point in even trying to explain any more; he was past listening. It was stamped on those hard features, turning his eyes opaque with disgust. And the truth was that Emily couldn't wait to get out of there. The sooner she could get miles away from here, the better. She wanted to hide away from the world, lick her wounds, try to forget that last night had ever happened...

But before she could do that, there was one thing she needed to know.

'Still here?' Vito goaded darkly. 'I told you to get out.'

'Not till you tell me what she—what Ruth said.'

His dark head went back, deep grey eyes narrowing sharply.

'You care? Isn't it a little late to develop a conscience—or even any interest in this?'

But Emily had had enough of his tormenting.

'Tell me!' she flung at him. 'Just tell me and I'll be gone.'

He threw up his hands in what in anyone else would have been a gesture of defeat, but which from Vito looked like total exasperation.

'She said that your husband had been asking about you and that you'd better get yourself back there before he really started to wonder where you were. And if you were wondering whether I told her that you were with me—in my bed, on a one-night stand—then no, I thought I'd leave that to you and your conscience…if you have one.'

But Emily wasn't listening.

Mark had been asking about her. Vito had no idea what those words did to her. The way they had made her feel.

When had Mark asked about her? *How* had he asked about her? And, perhaps more importantly, *who* was he asking about?

Whirling round, she bent over the tumble-drier, yanked at the door.

Her jeans were dry at least but that was all that she could say about them. They were crumpled beyond belief, the last few moments in the stalled drier only adding to the mess the sea water and a night on the floor had made of them.

But Emily didn't care. She couldn't care. All that mattered to her was getting into her clothes as quickly as possible and getting out of here. Wrenching the waist button open, pulling down the still-hot zip, she scrambled into the trousers, hopping slightly on the floor as she pulled them up. She was fastening the waistband when she realised that Vito was still there. Still leaning against the wall, still watching her.

Strangely she felt far more nervous, far more shy at being watched getting *dressed* than she had ever felt getting undressed or appearing totally naked in the night.

'I thought you were going to take a shower,' she flung at him and saw his mouth quirk into a cold, cruel smile.

Black eyes flicked over her, looking her up and down. There wasn't a glimmer of light in them, not a sliver of warmth.

But then last night had been so very, very different. Vito had been different. Nothing was the same now as it had been then. And in spite of herself she felt the hot burn of tears in her eyes, felt her vision blur at the thought of what she had lost.

'I'm intrigued,' Vito drawled cynically,

'watching this transformation from good-time girl to devoted wife hurrying home to her husband right in front of my eyes. Does he believe in this— your husband?' he added. 'Is the poor fool convinced that you are his loving spouse and not the *puttana* you really are?'

It was just what she needed. A moment before she had felt herself weakening, felt pathetic, foolish tears threatening, and she had almost given herself away in front of this cold-faced, colder-eyed monster. But the lash of his cruel words, the deliberate insult he had slid in like a stiletto between her ribs had pulled her up short. It had stiffened her backbone, made her draw herself up to face him. She even, totally surprising herself, managed a flash of a smile that she prayed looked careless and unconcerned.

'Perhaps I don't care,' she tossed at him, bringing up her chin and meeting that stony-eyed gaze with a courage she was very far from feeling. Not that her voice betrayed her, she was glad to hear. 'Perhaps the risks are part of the excitement. Part of the fun.'

That had wiped the sneer from his face, she was delighted to see. If she had thrown something nasty and very slimy right in his face, his head couldn't have gone back more swiftly, his expression changing to one of appalled shock just for a moment before he collected himself again and the blazing contempt was back.

'Perhaps—'

'Shut up!' Vito exploded, disgust dripping from the words. 'Shut up, damn you!'

'What's wrong, Vito?'

Somehow Emily managed to control her quivering chin, the tongue that seemed to have tangled itself up in knots.

'Don't you like it when a woman plays you at your own game?'

For the space of a couple of unsteady and uneven heartbeats she thought she'd gone too far. The blaze of black fury in his eyes had her taking an uneasy step backwards, watching him warily.

But then Vito obviously regained control of the temper that had almost slipped away from him. He swore again, more bitterly this time and pushed himself upright, raking both hands through the thick darkness of his hair.

'I'm going for that shower,' he told her, his voice raw with angry disgust. 'You'd better not be here when I get out.'

'Oh, I won't be,' she assured him. 'I promise you I won't.'

And then, because he had turned his back and was walking away and she couldn't see his stunning face or the violent anger that had stamped the harsh white lines on it, she said, 'I don't want to hang around, you see—my husband's waiting for me to come home to him and tell him all about it.'

The only response was the sound of a door slamming hard, shutting her off from any sight or sound of Vito. He was gone. She would never see him again. But even so she was weak enough to wait until she heard the sound of the shower, the noise of the water pounding down in the small bathroom, to admit to herself that it was time to go. And this time she didn't need to try to hold back the tears that flowed down her cheeks as she headed towards the door.

She barely saw the road as she almost ran to the car, stumbling awkwardly in the shoes she had rammed onto her feet. She didn't see her surroundings, the sand and the sea, because of the bitter tears that burned in her eyes.

In the car she had to take a few moments to compose herself. To draw on the inner strength that had got her so far but now, today, was coming so close to breaking. She sat with her hands clenched tightly around the steering wheel, skin stretched taut, as she fought with the tears that distorted her vision. She couldn't drive like this; she just wouldn't be safe. The end of the road seemed to dance before her unfocused eyes, the white line down its centre blurred into the tarmac, and all the other cars parked along the edge of the street seemed just a blend of colours, no defined shapes.

She had to get a grip on herself. Mark had been asking for her. She had to get back to him.

And Vito Corsentino wanted nothing to do with her. She'd made sure of that with the way she'd lied, embroidering her story until he believed she was little more than a tramp. So there was no point at all in staying here. He wouldn't want to see her again and if he did then he would only savage her again, making the pain so much worse.

And what had she lost after all?

Reality forced her to ask herself the question as the memory of the cold, contemptuous look on Vito's face when she had last seen him, the recollection of the way that he had turned from her in disgust, threatened to destroy completely what little was left of her composure. If the truth was told it had been nothing but a one-night stand and no more. Thousands of women experienced the same, enjoyed the experience and then moved on without letting it destroy them.

She was only deluding herself to imagine that she had felt so much more. That it could have meant more. But the truth was that she had felt as if she was being ripped in two as she had fled out the door of Vito's flat and heard it slam behind her. And the worst part had been knowing that he had still been there, almost within reach. But he had been in the bathroom, in the shower with the water pulsing down onto his naked, beautiful male body.

Emily curled one hand into a tight fist and brought it down hard on the edge of the steering wheel, trying to force the memories of the night and the feel of that glorious, hard-muscled body close to hers, invading hers, from her mind. He had been able to do that without a second's hesitation. Even now he was in his shower, washing away all trace of her from his body, the scent of her from his skin—and the image of her from his thoughts.

There was no future there and she had only been fantasising by allowing herself to imagine it.

Her future wasn't here. She didn't know where it was, only that it didn't lie with Vito Corsentino in a small, shabby flat beside the sea. For a few brief, shining moments she might have dreamed that that was how it could be but reality had soon taught her that it would never be that way.

She had no idea what future did lie ahead of her. But at least the one night she had spent with Vito had given her the belief that there could be a future for her somewhere out there. Somewhere, out beyond the misery and despair of the past years there had to be something better for her.

But first she had to deal with the present, with whatever was waiting for her at home and get through that.

Sighing, she pushed the key into the ignition and turned it, hearing the engine roar. She allowed herself one last, lingering look down onto the beach, where the sunlit sea now lapped lazily at the shore, no trace at all of the wild, swirling waves that the wind had whipped up on the day before. In the night the tide had come up right to the promenade wall so that even the traces of footprints, hers and Vito's, had been totally erased from the damp sand.

It was as if they had never been.

And in just the same way, her memory would be wiped from Vito's mind, she told herself as she let out the brake and swung the small car slowly into the road to join the flow of the traffic heading out of town. She would be completely forgotten, not even the vaguest image of their meeting ever stirring the surface of his mind.

And she should do the same. It would be best for her, wisest—safest to forget, or at least pretend to herself that Vito had never happened.

That was what she should do. But the sudden, twisting pain that tore at her heart as she indicated, turned left and headed up the steep hill away from the shore warned her that what she *should* do and what she could actually manage to do were two very different things.

CHAPTER EIGHT

WHAT the hell was he doing here?

Vito brought his car to a halt, yanked on the brake with less than his usual care, and stared at the house straight in front of him.

When he had imagined himself turning up at Emily Lawton's home at any time after their brief encounter, he hadn't really thought ahead to what he might find or where she might live. But if he had thought of her home, then it would not have been this large, elegant stone-built manor house that came to mind.

Oh, face it! Realising that the engine was still idling, he reached out and switched it off with a brusque twist of his wrist. The truth was that he had never, ever imagined seeing Emily again, let alone thought of turning up at her home, unannounced and unprepared. Hell, hadn't he spent the past almost five months trying to forget that the damn woman ever existed?

And that was the trouble.

He'd *tried. Dannazione,* but he'd tried. He'd thrown himself into his work, but each time he carved a new piece he'd found that unless he concentrated fiercely he would end up carving her face or her hands, or her body...

He'd tried to see other women. But no woman appealed—or if he did find a spark of interest, it was because of a tall, slender figure, or a head of sleek blonde hair—blue eyes. There were times when he'd been tempted to take another woman to bed. To lose himself in pleasure, drive away the memory of a single night that lingered in his mind like paint in water after a brush had been washed out, colouring everything and impossible to remove. But he had never been able to bring himself to actually make the move.

In the end he had been glad to get back to Sicily. Glad to go back to the life he had taken a year's holiday from. He had planned to concentrate on being Corsentino of Corsentino Marine and Leisure but then some news he had picked up while in England and had passed on to his brother, Guido, had had reverberations that he had never anticipated.

'Emily Lawton,' he murmured, speaking aloud at last the name that he had refused to let pass his lips again until the shock discovery yesterday had forced it out into the open.

Emily Lawton.

He could have found her, hunted her down, if he'd wanted to. And if he was honest, he'd been tempted. But when he came close to weakening then the memory of what she'd done, of the way she'd behaved—the fact that she was *married*—had slammed the door in his mind shut on any such foolish idea and kept his thoughts from wandering on to the possibility of how it might be if they met again.

But then Guido had gone to England to stop a marriage and had ended up bringing home the bride for himself. And his brother's new woman—Amber—had known who Emily Lawton was. In fact, Emily had been a guest at the aborted wedding. She'd fainted when she'd seen Guido enter the church.

Fainted because she'd thought that Guido was *him*.

And then later she had seen Guido in the hotel. And gone as white as a sheet, his brother had said. Again because she'd believed that Guido was him.

Or because she'd feared exposure, the cynically realistic part of his mind inserted sharply.

But no, that didn't work. Why should the story he had to tell matter now? Her husband was dead, so there was no spouse to be shattered by the revelation. And besides, if the foul things she had flung at him the last time he saw her had been true then her husband had already known—and liked knowing about the sorts of things she got up to.

Nausea assailed him at the thought, the memory a foul taste in his mouth.

Which brought him back to his original question. What the hell was he doing here?

It wasn't even twenty-four hours since he had heard Amber speak Emily's name and already he was here on her doorstep, unable to stay away. He had been home and packing his bag, ordering the jet, within thirty minutes of finding out where she lived, unable to think beyond the fact that he couldn't rest until he came face to face with her. The plane had been in the air two hours later.

He had vowed to himself—and to her—that he never, ever wanted to see this woman again. So why the devil was he here?

He was still struggling to find an answer to that question when he noticed a movement in one of the ground-floor windows. A pale face, blonde head, a slender figure. A female figure. From this distance it was impossible to make out any details, see her face clearly, but he didn't have to see to know it was Emily.

And immediately he knew why he had come.

Just the brief sight of her like that, a face in a window, kicked every sense he possessed up several notches, heading straight for overdrive. His thoughts were flooded with the recollection of the way she had felt to touch, to kiss, to taste. The memory of the softness of her skin, the sweet warmth of her body and how it had been underneath him, the way that she had opened to him, the moist heat of her enclosing him, set his heart pounding, the blood racing through his veins until his head spun and his mouth dried, heat throbbing between his legs.

Just to see her from a distance made him hard and hungry in the space of a heartbeat and the hunger was the sensation that had never left him in all the months they had been apart.

And *that* was why he was here now.

That one night had not been enough. It had stayed in his mind ever since. He had hated her for the deception she had practised on him and he still detested even the thought of it. He had despised himself for the fact that he could not get her out of his thoughts, but even after all this time she was still there like an itch he could not scratch. But while she was married he would never, ever touch her.

But she wasn't married any more. And that changed everything.

Emily had heard the car come up the drive and halt outside the front door. The estate agent was a little early. The appointment had been for eleven; it was barely ten-thirty yet. Not that she minded. The sooner she got this over with, the better; then she could hope to move on with her life.

Sighing, she got up from the chair where she'd been sitting and smoothed down her dress. It was unexpectedly warm for spring and she had had to hunt for something to wear to fit the temperature. Luckily the flowing lines of blue and green print were very forgiving as well as being cool and comfortable.

A quick glance in the mirror made her grimace in distaste. In spite of the extra care she'd taken with her make-up that morning, knowing she was going to be on public view, she still looked pale and rather wan. Her hair needed cutting too. It had grown out of the sleek bob that had been so easy to keep up and now was frankly a mess. But she hadn't had the time or the energy to care about such things.

The truth was that she was tired. Tired and low. So much had happened in the last five months that she almost felt like a totally different person. She didn't even recognise the Emily who had spent one wild, irresponsible night in a small flat beside the…

'No!'

She shook her head firmly to distract herself, refusing to let her mind go back to that one night, that one man.

He'd haunted her for far too long. In the day, things weren't too bad. She had so much to do, so much to worry about, that she managed to focus her thoughts on that and distract herself through the daylight hours. But in the lonely darkness she'd lost hours of the night trying not to think about him. Even more hours thinking about him. And when she had finally fallen into fitful sleep, the hot, erotic dreams that had plagued her had made her restless and uneasy, waking bathed in sweat, her heart racing and her breath coming in ragged, uneven gasps.

Perhaps when this final stage of the official process that had followed Mark's death was over, she could go away somewhere quiet and get away from everything. Try to forget. But of course there was one good reason why she could never *really* forget.

A gentle palm stroked the spot on her lower body where a faint swell revealed yet another reason for her tiredness. And for the fact that she could never, ever truly forget Vito Corsentino. Underneath her hand lay the almost-five-month pregnancy that had resulted from her one night of passion with the seductive Sicilian, a permanent legacy from the brief time they had shared. Vito Corsentino's baby. The child that was almost all she would be left with once the formal legalities were over and she started her new life—as a single mother.

Why hadn't the doorbell rung? Surely Joe McKenzie must have reached the house by now? Or perhaps he was already surveying the property from the outside.

Emily went to the window, pulled back the lace curtain very slightly and peered out, blinking at the brightness of the sun.

Strange. He was still in the car. A brand-new car from the look of it; certainly one she had never seen before. Business at McKenzie and Watson must be doing very well.

But there was no point in him sitting out there when he could be getting on with the job he'd come to do.

Hurrying to the door, she pulled it open, fixing a smile on her face as she turned towards the sleek silver-grey vehicle and shaded her eyes with her hands.

'You don't have to wait there till eleven, Joe. I know you're a little early but it really doesn't matter.'

The sun was shining straight into her eyes so that all she could see was that dark, masculine figure in the driving seat. For a moment her heart fluttered uncertainly as she wondered if in fact this was really Joe. But hastily she caught herself up, telling herself it was just the effect of the sun that turned the man in the car into a black silhouette behind the smoked glass of the windows. She had been letting her memories haunt her again and now she was being fanciful.

'Would you like to come in and have a cup of coffee?'

The silence and the stillness of the man in the car was disturbing. Had Joe sent someone else? Or…

Unwillingly her thoughts went back to the previous weekend. She had attended the wedding of one of her husband's cousins and in the middle of the ceremony the door at the back of the church had opened and a man had walked in.

A tall, dark, devastating man. A man who looked so much like Vito Corsentino that for a moment she had thought that he was him. She'd believed that somehow, God knew how, the man she had shared that one passionate night with had found her. He had hunted her down and had come to the wedding to confront her.

The small village church had spun round her. She'd felt as if the walls were closing in, there was no air and she could hardly breathe. Her eyes had closed and she had fallen from her seat in a dead faint. When she had come round, she was outside, where two friends had carried her. And the dark stranger was nowhere to be seen.

But she'd met up with him again later.

'Joe?'

Her voice was more uncertain now, taking on a tremor of apprehension. *Was* this Joe McKenzie? Or someone else, come to disturb the hard-won peace she'd finally found for herself?

Cautiously she took a step forward then, re-thinking, froze into stillness again. She didn't want to put too much space between herself and the doorway. What if her imagination was not playing her tricks? What if she should really be…?

The thoughts died inside her head as there was movement from the car, the driver's door swinging open. A hand appeared on the top of the door. A long-fingered, tanned hand. The sort of hand that the well past middle-aged and decidedly plump Joe McKenzie had never had.

The sort of hand that made Emily's heart stop dead in shock just to see it.

'No…' It escaped from her in a low, desperate whisper. 'Please God—no!'

But her prayers were not answered. She could only watch in horror, feeling all the warmth of the day ebb away as she saw the broad shoulders, the jet-black hair that gleamed in the bright sunlight, the handsome face of the man she had thought she would never see again. He was dressed much more formally than the other times she had seen him, the sleekly tailored lines of the light grey suit he wore with a pale blue shirt hugging the powerful body, emphasising his height and strength in a way that made her throat uncomfortably dry.

Those deep grey eyes were hidden behind sunglasses but as he stood up and stretched lazily, easing the stiffness of his journey, he took off the concealing lenses and slanted a swift, narrow-eyed glance at her stunned face.

'*Ciao, belleza,*' he drawled with the sort of smile that made the earth seem to tilt beneath her feet. 'Good afternoon, Signora Lawton. It's a pleasure to see you again.'

'No.'

It was all she could manage. And she actually brought up her hand, holding it out as if to ward off something nasty that she feared was heading towards her.

'No, *cara?*' Vito echoed, his tone turning that *'cara'* into something that was light-years away from the true meaning of the word. 'You think I did not mean that? Well, let me assure you that, no matter how I happen to feel about you, it is always a pleasure to see your lovely face.'

'It's what you feel about me that bothers me,' Emily stammered, so totally confused by that 'your lovely face' that she didn't know at all how to react. 'I know exactly how you do feel about me—you made it bitterly clear the last time I saw you. And, that being so, I really can't understand what you're doing here.'

'I brought you this.'

Putting his hand into the pocket of his jacket, he pulled out a small blue coin purse, which he held out towards her.

'My parking-money purse. I wondered where it had got to. But why wait all this time to get it back to me?'

After all, she doubted if the purse held more than a coin or two.

'I didn't know where you lived before now.'

'But you could have found out.'

'I could…' Vito nodded thoughtfully. 'But even if I knew where to find you, there was a very good reason why I should stay away.'

'And now?'

'Now that reason no longer exists.'

He was giving nothing away. The shaded glass might no longer be concealing his eyes from her but the deep dark gaze was almost as opaque as the tinted glass had been.

'My sympathy on the death of your husband.' It was stiffly formal, impeccably polite. And it forced from her an equally stiff acknowledgement.

'Thank you. Unfortunately it was not unexpected.'

Even after four months, she still found it difficult to accept any comments, or, worse, any sympathy on Mark's death. She had no idea how she was expected to behave.

'But how…?' She let the question fade away as realisation dawned. 'Of course—the man at the St Clair wedding.'

'My brother,' Vito confirmed. 'Or, rather, Amber, who I believe was supposed to have been the bride at that event.'

'You've seen Amber?'

For a moment Emily was diverted. The disruption of Rafe St Clair's wedding had been the talk of the town for the past week. The St Clair family had made sure that everyone knew how appalled and insulted they'd been and poor Amber Wellesley's name had been mud in every conversation she'd heard. But of the missing bride herself there had been no sign.

'She's with Guido—in Sicily.'

'Sicily is—is that where your brother lives?'

'It's where I live too. The flat was just a temporary base while I was in England.'

I know—I went there and the place was empty—closed up. She had to swallow down the words, fighting not to let them escape. When she had found out that she was pregnant—a realisation that had been delayed by the event of Mark's death and everything else that had piled on top of her at the time—she had made one weak, lonely trip to the flat. Vito had at least the right to know that he had fathered a child. She had resigned herself to the fact that he would probably not even be interested. What she hadn't expected was to find that he had packed and gone and there was no one who seemed to know where.

There was something that was not quite right with what Vito was saying, something was fretting at her thoughts—until it was completely knocked out of her head by Vito's sudden move forward.

'What are you doing?'

It was too high, too sharp, and gave away too much about the fear that was bubbling up inside her at another sudden and unwanted realisation. The dress she was wearing was loose and flowing, swirling around her with any slight movement. But, realising that she had her arms folded across her body in a way that pressed the loose dress against her, she hastily unfolded them again.

Just for the moment Vito might not have noticed the difference in her shape, the way that her waist was practically non-existent with the extra weight.

Her actual 'bump' might still be very small but if he came any closer…

'You offered me coffee.'

The look he turned on her said that her question had only amused him. He clearly didn't think it was meant to be taken at all seriously.

'I'd appreciate a cup—thank you.'

'But that wasn't you!'

She really must get a grip on herself. She was revealing far too much in the way that she spoke, making it plain that there was something wrong, something she wanted to hide from him—something more than just not wanting him in her home.

But the truth was that her mind was anywhere but on the conversation she was actually having.

'I mean—I didn't invite *you* in for coffee! I thought you were Joe.'

'And Joe is?' Vito enquired, his personal opinion of just who Joe might be written in the cold contempt in his eyes, all trace of amusement totally erased in an instant.

'Not what you're thinking!' Emily flashed back at him. 'Joe is the local estate agent. He's coming to value the house.'

'You're selling up?'

That was a surprise, Vito admitted. When he had arrived at the house, on his way up the long, curving drive, he had thought that it was obvious why Emily had been so keen to get back to her husband after the night they had spent together. She had taken a good look at the small, shabby flat he lived in and fled straight back home to the comfort and luxury her marriage could offer.

'I have to.' The words came out on an odd note, one that he couldn't interpret.

'You can't afford the upkeep, is that it? I would have thought from all this that your husband...'

A glacial glare from those soft blue eyes froze him out before he could finish the sentence.

'You know nothing about my husband,' Emily declared. 'So I'll thank you to keep out of things that are none of your business.'

He'd touched a nerve there, that was obvious. But pressing her further would only make her close up again even more. He'd bide his time and see what he could discover later. There was some-thing to discover, something she was hiding, he was sure of that.

And there was something different about her

features seen up close. There was a glow to her cheeks and her hair, and the thin, rather drawn look had disappeared. She didn't look like a woman who had been mourning her husband.

'So are you going to invite me in or not?'

Not, it seemed from the way her face changed, her jaw tightening, her eyes narrowing. Deliberately Vito switched to a charm offensive, holding that sapphire gaze and smiling straight into her suspicious eyes.

'Come, now, *cara,* you surely wouldn't begrudge me a coffee when I've travelled all this way to see you.'

'All this way?' she scoffed. 'It's hardly sixty miles. And I am not your darling. You made that very plain the last time you saw me.'

Vito ignored that final remark, concentrating instead on her first comment.

'Believe me, I've come a lot further than those sixty miles.'

'From the coast?'

'No, from Sicily.'

He had her now. She looked stunned, her head going back and her mouth falling slightly open in shock.

'From—Sicily?'

'*Si,* from Siracusa, to be exact. Where do you think I saw your friend Amber?'

'I thought—I thought…'

She shook her head slowly, bewilderment clouding her eyes.

'But you're not going to say that you've come from Sicily today…I don't believe you!' she protested when he nodded an answer to her question.

'I flew overnight, then drove here from the airport. The last time I had coffee was on the plane. So, how about it, *cara,* hmm?' he cajoled. 'What harm can one cup of coffee do?'

For a moment he thought that she was going to refuse. Suspicion and hostility still radiated from her so that he almost felt that he could see the small hairs on the back of her neck standing up like those of a wary cat faced with an unknown intruder into its territory.

But there was curiosity there too. She was intrigued and more than a little flattered to think that he had come all this way to see her. He almost had her hooked.

All he had to do was to keep silent now and…

'One cup of coffee, then,' she said slowly, reluctantly. 'And that's it.'

She had already turned, heading back towards the house, and so didn't see the gleam of triumph in Vito's eyes as he followed her.

One coffee—and that would definitely *not* be it.

One coffee was just the start of what he had in mind.

CHAPTER NINE

'ALL right, Vito, I think this has gone on long enough.'

Emily prayed that the way she spoke didn't reveal just how hard she had had to work to bring herself to actually get the words out into the open. Twice already she had told herself that she needed to say something; that she needed to ask questions, and, hopefully, get some answers. She couldn't just leave things in limbo like this. But twice already she had also backed down, losing her nerve at the very last minute.

She made the coffee, thanking heaven fervently for the fact that the violent reaction she had had in the first months of her pregnancy, when even the smell of the drink had made her stomach heave, had now eased. She still didn't like the taste of coffee one little bit, but she could make a pot for Vito, pour it into a mug and place it in front of him without actually throwing up. And he didn't appear to notice that she only got a glass of water for herself, or if he did, it didn't bother him in any way.

They'd made a sort of conversation as Vito enjoyed his drink. A strange, inane, going nowhere, not really saying anything sort of conversation that meandered from trivial topic to pointless topic only to fill the silence that would otherwise be too heavy to breathe, too thick with tension to endure a moment longer.

They'd talked about the weather, for heaven's sake! About how unexpectedly dry and warm it was for April, the chance that it might rain later, and the fact that the gardens needed the water. They'd talked about his flight, his drive from the airport to the house, the state of the roads, until Emily was just about ready to scream with frustration and near panic.

If she had been talking to a complete stranger, making polite conversation in a lift or a train compartment, it would have been bad enough. But she couldn't look at Vito, lounging comfortably in the big black leather armchair, his long legs stretched out in front of him, booted feet crossed at the ankles, and not *remember*.

If he turned his head so that the sunlight caught

on the gleaming blue-black strands of his hair, she remembered how it had felt to have those strands under her fingertips when she had reached up to curl her hands around the strong bones of his skull. If he looked at her she recalled the way those dark grey eyes had looked down into hers as she lay beneath him; how they had sometimes been almost feverish with passion or at other times glazed with lazy desire. When he lifted his mug to drink she felt her own mouth soften at the memory of how it had felt to have those beautifully shaped lips crush hers or tantalise with gentle, teasing kisses, the taste of his tongue so vivid in her mouth that it was as if those kisses had only been five minutes ago, not five months.

And when he moved his hands, to smooth back a lock of jet hair that had fallen over his wide forehead, or tug his elegant silk tie loose at the throat, she felt her body prickle all over with heat at the most sensual memories of all. The thought of how those long, bronzed fingers had once caressed her skin, teased her senses awake, brought her such stunning pleasure, made every inch of her sting with remembered need and the longing to experience it all over again.

And the knowledge that she could never know

that delight again, that such pleasure was one she must always deny herself now and in the future, was what finally pushed the words from her mouth before she had a chance to try to hold them back.

'It's time we talked.'

'*Naturalamente, carina,*' Vito smiled, replacing his mug on the coffee-table with what she felt was deliberately excessive care. 'What is it you want to talk about?'

It was all completely wrong, Emily told herself as she tried to imagine the scene viewed by someone outside the window, looking in. If they did then they would get exactly the opposite impression to the reality of the situation.

Seeing Vito looking so relaxed and at ease, his head resting against the back of the chair, his hands lying carelessly on the broad square-cut arms, any casual observer would think that he was the one at home here. That the house belonged to him. While she, perched on the edge of the settee, her legs pressed tightly together, feet flat on the ground and her back stiffly upright, her hand clamped tightly around the almost untouched glass of water, must look like a nervous stranger in her own home.

'You know very well what I want to talk about.'

His lazy question was infuriating, making her fingers tighten on her glass until she almost expected it to shatter under the pressure.

'I want you to explain what you're doing here— why you came—and don't tell me that you came to return my parking-money purse and the single pound coin it happens to have in it,' she put in hastily as he opened his mouth to give her some obviously flippant answer. 'Because I know that's just not the truth. No one would make a special journey from the next village to bother with something as small as that, let alone fly here from Sicily of all places!'

'You're right,' Vito stunned her by agreeing, so much so that she felt her mouth actually fall open in surprise and hastily clamped it shut again, painfully aware of how foolish she must look gaping at him like that.

'I'm…?' She couldn't find the strength to finish the question.

'You're quite right,' Vito confirmed again, his tone astoundingly mild and easy. He even smiled. The sort of smile that hit her straight in the eyes and made her feel as if she had been struck by a brilliant flash of steel-grey lightning, one that sizzled all the way down her spine until it made her toes curl up tightly inside her soft leather shoes. 'I didn't come to return the purse—that, of course, was just an excuse.'

So now they were coming to it. Now she would find out what he really planned. It was what she'd said she wanted, what she had been trying to convince herself she must ask from the moment she'd realised that he was the man in the car and not Joe McKenzie. And she did want to know what his answer was going to be, but that didn't stop her mouth from drying painfully, her throat tightening until she felt she could hardly get a breath past the knot that had formed deep inside.

'What...?'

Her voice croaked painfully as she tried to get the word out, but she didn't dare to lift her glass, sip at the water to ease the raw sensation for fear that her hand would shake so badly with tension that she might spill it all over herself like a fool.

'What is the real reason, then?'

'Isn't it obvious? I came for you.'

'Oh, come on! I don't believe that! You're even less likely to want to come all this way to see me—when the last time I saw you you made it very very plain that...'

The words faded, died, as she met his eyes and saw the way he was looking at her. Saw the cool, assessing gaze, the faint shake of his head that told her she was not saying the right thing; that she had got something totally wrong.

Nervously she tried to think back over what she had said, what he had said before that. Slowly, horrifyingly, realisation dawned in the same moment that Vito left her in no room for doubt by spelling it out calmly and deliberately.

'I didn't say I came to see you—I came for you.'

Emily had the disturbing feeling that if she could she would have pushed herself up from the settee and turned and run, getting as far as possible from this man and the claim he was making on her. But even though her pregnancy didn't show too much yet, she already felt less supple and a lot less light on her feet than normal, so she didn't dare to try and make any rash movements.

'For…'

This time she didn't gape, this time her mouth didn't fall open even though the shock was every bit as great as when he had casually announced the fact that returning her purse was only an excuse for being here. This time her lips clamped tight shut on the explosion of disbelief that almost escaped her and she bit her tongue hard rather than let out what she really meant to say.

'Just what is that supposed to mean?' she managed at last.

'What do you think it means?'

Vito leaned back in his chair again, watching the swift, revealing play of emotions cross her face like clouds scudding in front of the sun. She was stunned, fine—he'd expected that—but what else would those expressive features reveal?

He knew she'd put on a play of rejection—a pretence of denying the passion that still burned between them. But it would be a pretence. She hadn't forgotten him any more than he had been able to put her out of his mind. He'd seen that flare of instant recognition in her eyes when he had first got out of the car, caught the spark of response that she had been unable to hide.

'I thought my meaning was perfectly clear.'

'Not to me!'

The sudden rush of colour to her cheeks, the way those challenging eyes dropped, not quite able to meet his, told their own story. But still it seemed she was determined to keep up the pretence for a while longer.

'Signor Corsentino—'

'Vito,' he inserted smoothly. 'I like the way it sounds on your tongue.'

That earned him another furious glare, one so ridiculously fierce that it made his mouth twitch, wanting to break into a smile. But he controlled it with an effort. If she thought he was laughing at her then she would become even more incandescent with rage, and, fun though it might be to play the game that way, he didn't feel that he had the patience to spend time trying to calm her down.

Simply being in the room with her had strained his self-control to the limit. Every time she had moved he had caught a faint waft of her scent, a blend of something floral and the soft, intoxicating aroma of her skin. And just inhaling it had sent a sensual message fizzing through every nerve in his body, awakening the hunger that had always tormented him when he had remembered that single night in his flat.

But now it wasn't memories that filled his mind but the reality of physical hunger. A hunger he was having to fight to control.

'Vito, I don't have time to play games—I'm expecting a visitor soon.'

Dannazione, he'd forgotten about the estate

agent. When she'd thought he was the man she was expecting, she'd said something about eleven and it was quarter-to now. He was going to have to play this slightly differently from the way he had originally planned.

'This isn't a game, *belleza*. Believe me, I was never more serious in my life.'

'And you are going to have to believe *me* when I say that I don't know what you're talking about.'

'Liar!' Vito reproved softly. 'You know very well that we have unfinished business between us.'

'No...'

She shook her head determinedly, sending the fine blonde hair flying around her face.

'No!'

'Yes.'

He was sitting forward now, dark eyes locking with cloudy blue, and he saw the way that her gaze widened, the revealing rise and fall of her breasts as her breathing quickened, grew uneven. She was giving herself away in so many ways, her body giving off messages that were the opposite of what her mouth was saying.

'You wanted to know why I came here—what brought me to your door today. Well, the truth is that I couldn't help myself. I couldn't stay away.'

He'd caught her now, had her held like a deer in the headlights of a car, her pupils huge and black so that barely a rim of the soft blue showed around the edges. She wasn't aware of the way that she had moved, that she was matching his pose, leaning towards him as he spoke, her gaze intent on his face, her hands open on her lap, no longer clasped together and twisting tight.

'I haven't been able to get you out of my mind since you left that morning—and I know you've felt the same.'

'I've what?'

The arrogance of the man! Emily couldn't believe what she was hearing. Did he really believe…?

'I've done no such thing!'

Oh, dear, did the vehemence of her tone give away the fact that she was lying through her teeth?

'Just what makes you think…?'

'I don't think—I know,' Vito declared with such supreme confidence that if she hadn't been sitting down she had the nasty feeling that his assertion would have taken all the strength from her legs and dropped her down onto the settee, unable to support herself. 'It was there in your face when you first saw me, when you realised who it was in the car.'

'It was no such thing! You're kidding yourself!'

She expected another assured response. Another declaration that he knew what he was talking about, and she was prepared to deny it till she was blue in the face—but what knocked her sideways mentally, took the breath from her lungs, was the fact that he did no such thing. In fact he said nothing. Nothing at all. Just gave her another of those long, considering looks, the ones that seemed to see right into her mind— into her heart, her soul—and read what was there, no matter how hard she tried to conceal it from him.

So had she? Had she really been so transparent that she had somehow given him a clue to the thoughts that had tormented her in the five months since she had seen him? Had she shown something of the lonely days, the even lonelier nights she had spent remembering and wondering?

Had there been all that in her face? Had the cruel twist of her heart when she'd recognised him put some light in her eyes that he'd been able to interpret as a welcome?

'Don't!'

'What?'

She started violently as Vito suddenly moved

forward, taking her chin in one hand and pressing his thumb against her bottom lip.

'Don't do that…'

It was only then that she realised how she had been worrying at her bottom lip, expressing the wild confusion inside her by digging her teeth into the softness of her flesh. But now Vito's thumb had taken the place of her teeth, smoothing softly over the skin, erasing the damage she had done to herself.

And it felt soothing. It felt gentle. It felt good—too good. More than good: it felt dangerously wonderful.

The scent of his skin was in her nostrils. The taste of his skin was on her lips; if she let her tongue slide out, she could savour it there too. And Vito must have moved because suddenly he was so much closer. He was right on the edge of his chair, his knees almost touching hers. His face seemed only inches away from hers, his eyes so deep and dark she felt she could drown in them. Every time he blinked she felt sure that she should feel a breeze from the way that those lush black lashes swept the air.

She could see the faint shadow of his beard under his skin and her fingers itched to reach out and touch, feel the contrast between the roughness of stubble and the warm satin smoothness of his skin. She could hear the soft sound of his breathing, almost sense the heavy, regular beat of his heart, and when he swallowed she watched the movement of his bronzed throat with an almost hypnotic fascination, unable to drag her eyes away. And when she followed the movement down, down to where he had tugged loose his tie and opened the neck of his shirt she could see the way that the golden toned skin went further down, under the fine blue cotton, just a hint of dark, crisp hair shadowing in the V-necked opening.

'Vito…' It was barely a sound, just a breath escaping her lips, and when she spoke it her mouth closed around his caressing thumb once more, stilling the movement, tasting him again, savouring both the intimate flavour and the burning memories it brought back to her mind.

He was still only touching her on the mouth, still only connected to her in that one, small spot, and yet she felt as if he was surrounding her totally. As if he had enclosed her in his arms, pressed the heat and power of his body against her, covered her totally with his strength.

Because that was how she remembered it. How it had once been when he had rescued her, when he had swept her up into his arms and carried her away from the beach and she had gone to his bed so happily that she had forgotten about everything else in her life. Forgotten all the misery and the stress and known only that with this man, in his arms, she felt right and safe and happy.

And that was how she wanted to feel again. She needed to live that wonderful experience over again, if only one more time. She had to know his touch, his kiss, his caress. She had to know *him*.

'Vito…' she murmured again, her throat feeling thick with emotion, her eyes blurring as she swayed towards him slightly, unable to hold back.

'*Si, cara?*'

It was low and huskily intent, the beautiful accent heightened on the deep, rich tones, and he was so close that his breath was warm on her face as he formed the words so that they were a caress as well as a sound that teased at her senses.

'Kiss me…'

She didn't even have time to get the words out fully before he was suiting action to the words, taking away his thumb and replacing it with his mouth, kissing her hard, crushing the sound back down her throat.

And at the same time he was up and out of his

chair, fastening his hands around her arms, hauling her from her seat to crush her against him, holding her close with muscles of steel. His lips plundered hers, his tongue invading her mouth, taking the moist essence of her and making it his own, tasting her, savouring her, knowing her.

Emily gave herself up to him, feeling the heat lick along her veins at the speed and intensity of a forest fire taking hold of the dry undergrowth, the brittle leaves and twigs, and sending them roaring into a wild, unstoppable conflagration in just a couple of seconds. In the space of a heart-beat she'd lost all thought, lost all control, lost all care for whether this was wise or foolish. She didn't know and she didn't care. All she was aware of was the hunger she felt for Vito's kiss. The need for his touch, the yearning, demanding need that filled every nerve, tightened her breasts and pulsed, hot and heavy, between her legs.

I came for you...

I came for you...

Vito's arrogant declaration pounded in her thoughts like the wild refrain in some primitive music. It was all she could think and it was all she wanted to think. After long months of bitter lone-liness, months in which she had felt lost and adrift on a cruel sea of hostility and isolation, just to know that someone wanted her, that someone cared in any way at all was such a liberating sensation that it went straight to her head like a rush of the finest, most potent cognac. Her mind spun, her legs weakened and all she could do was abandon herself to Vito's strength and passion, let the flames of need burn away the scars that unhappy thoughts had left behind.

'You see,' Vito muttered against her mouth, 'this was how it was, how it can be again. That night we were together, I had the best damn sex of my life, and I want more. That's why I had to come for you.'

CHAPTER TEN

WAS it possible to love and hate in the same moment? Emily wondered.

Or perhaps—much more likely—what she really meant was, was it possible to crave and to detest in the same moment? Because that was what she was feeling right now. Her mind seemed to be splitting in two in the same second that her body was burning up crazily, fizzing with the wild electricity of yearning, physical need.

She *wanted* this—oh, *how* she wanted it. She was hungry for it with a need that went way beyond any sense of right or wrong, wise or foolish, safe or totally, completely soul-destroyingly dangerous. She had dreamed so much about this, remembered it both in her waking days and in her sleep. Moving into Vito's arms had been like coming home.

But coming home should not be so tempting, nor so dangerous. Coming home should feel *safe* and *secure* and safe and secure were the last two possible words that she connected with the situation she was in, the way she was feeling right now.

Bringing her hands up in a rush, she caught hold of Vito's face, held it still as she wrenched her mouth away from his, put her head back slightly so that she could see his face. He was still holding her so tightly that she could only move a few inches away, bending her back against his arm to try to focus on his hard-boned features. She was so close that all she could really focus on were those dark, deep eyes.

But at least he wasn't kissing her. When he kissed her she couldn't think, she could only feel. And right now she *had* to think. She had to decide. Was there any sort of future possible with this man? And was it a future filled with one of those conflicting feelings that had almost torn her in two just moments before? With hate or…?

No, she wouldn't, couldn't let herself think of the word 'love' in connection with this man. She had only known him a few short hours; barely a day, all told. Such a few short hours but he filled her mind and her thoughts like no one else ever had.

And she *needed* him. She *wanted* him. Even now her body was aching with the hunger for his touch that she was having to deny herself in order to be able to try to at least consider what options she had ahead of her.

I came for you… he had said. *I came for you…* He still wanted her. And he still wanted her *enough* to have travelled all this way from Sicily to be with her.

I haven't been able to get you out of my mind since you left that morning…

What woman wouldn't be thrilled to hear a man say those words? Especially a man like Vito Corsentino.

And, even though she was only prepared to admit it to herself, the truth was that he had been so right when he had said that she had felt the same. She could deny it to his face, but deep inside, in her heart, she knew that she had never been able to forget him, no matter how hard she had tried. And now he had only to touch her again, to kiss her once, and she had been lost, putty in his hands.

But she couldn't risk letting him know *how* lost she was. She was going to have to put up some sort of a fight, wasn't she? Or it would just be that first meeting all over again and he would think that he could do as he wanted with her.

The idea of Vito Corsentino doing just as he

wanted with her made delicious shivers feather along her nerves, making her tingle all over. And when he reached for her mouth again her senses cried out to her to give in, though her mind told her she ought to put on the brakes if she possibly could.

'Just a minute…'

Inserting her hand between their two mouths, she pressed her fingers against his lips, stopping the kiss but not subduing the sensual experience. The feel of his mouth under her hand was devastating, the softness of his lips, the warmth of his breath against her skin made her heart skip several beats and her own breath catch in her throat. No matter how much she tried to armour herself against the sexual net this man could weave around her simply by existing, it only took the slightest touch, the smallest kiss to push her close to the edge of total meltdown.

'What about this unfinished business between us?'

It seemed to take more strength than usual to push the words from her mouth. Her throat wanted to close over them; hold them back. The truth was that she didn't really want to dig too deeply.

'What do you really want?'

'I want you.'

The black eyes met hers over the tops of her

fingers and she felt as if the fires that burned in them would sear her skin, brand her as his like some slave girl of primitive times bought and marked as the king's personal property.

'If you want honesty, I didn't come here for a relationship—I came here because I want you back in my bed.'

It was as harsh as a slap in the face and it made her pull back, twisting away from him, moving halfway across the room and then stopping, moving behind a chair to shield herself from him.

'You think that that's the way to win me?'

The words were raw with the pain that burned inside but that she wouldn't let him see in her expression as she faced him defiantly, blue eyes locking with darkest grey until she could almost see the sparks of challenge that flew between them.

She could see herself reflected in his face too, or, rather, the way he was feeling about her, about the bravado she was showing. It was there in the glint in his eyes and in the faint curve that was back on his mouth. He didn't mind the defiance, in fact he was quite enjoying it. And what made her shiver in spite of the warmth of the sun on her back was the sudden realisation that perhaps in a way he knew more about her than she did about herself.

Slowly her hand crept out, touched the carved wooden back of the chair that she was keeping between them, and she suddenly had to ask herself whether the truth was that she was keeping it there to keep him from her. Or was the reality the fact that she was putting it in the way of her own need, the temptation to ignore all promptings of common sense and go back into his arms?

Honesty forced her to admit that if she followed her heart, that was what she wanted to do. She had the frightening feeling that it was exactly what he was expecting.

'You think that just declaring that you want me in your bed is enough to make me throw myself at you?'

'You did on the beach.'

Emily winced at the memory the pointed words had evoked. She didn't want to be reminded of the wild madness that had taken her over then. The way that she had ignored all common sense and thoughts of her own safety.

'I—wasn't myself then. I was under stress and I'd just almost drowned.'

And he'd rushed into the sea to rescue her. At a time when no one else gave a damn about what happened to her, the effect had been like a rush of potent spirit to her head. But she wasn't in that situation any more. So why did she still feel that she might do something every bit as foolish all over again?

'Do you want me to flatter you—to cajole—to tell you that I'm madly in love with you? Well, *mi perdoni,* I don't do flattery and I don't do seduction by lies. Not when I want something this much.'

'So what do you do?' She had to struggle to resist the enticing tug of that 'Not when I want something this much'. She was so weak and so low that just the thought of being wanted that much made her legs tremble, her muscles turning to water. 'What do you give a woman if you don't flatter?'

'Honesty.'

There was no warmth in the steely grey eyes, but there was something else. Something that in a gentler man she would have described as sincerity. But in Vito, the only word she could come up with was forthrightness. The one thing she was sure of was that she really had no reason at all to doubt that he meant what he said.

'I'm paying you the compliment of giving you total honesty.'

'And what do you expect in return?'

'The same sort of honesty. I can't hide the fact

that I want you. If you're not with me, I'm thinking about you. If you are with me I can't take my eyes off you.'

It was like balm to her wounded soul. It soothed the death by a thousand cuts that Mark had inflicted on her. For Mark she hadn't been sexy enough, wasn't proactive enough in bed. She didn't give enough, he'd said at the beginning, she was too restrained, too controlled. By the end, the accusation had been that she was just plain frigid, a frosty, unfeminine bitch. Vito had shown her that none of those accusations were the truth. With him she had little or no control; any frost in her make-up had melted in the blaze of heat that flooded through her when he touched her.

'Honesty from you would be for you to admit that you want this too.'

'I do…' It was a long-drawn-out sigh, one she could no longer hold back. 'I do.'

Had she moved or had he? She suspected that they had acted simultaneously, taking a step— several steps nearer to each other so that all she had to do was to reach out a hand…

When she did so she found it taken into his, the warmth and strength of his clasp wonderful after the emptiness of the past few months.

Gently but irresistibly Vito drew her towards him, his arms coming round her as he bent his head to take her mouth again. He took his time about this kiss, lingering over the pleasure of teasing her, tasting her, enticing her to open up to him. And the explosion of heat that ran up her veins, setting the pathways of her nerves alight, instantly made total nonsense of Mark's vicious, belittling accusations.

Her breasts felt tight and swollen, her heartbeat setting up a heavy, honeyed pounding that was echoed in the throbbing pulse between her legs. Her eyes seemed weighted down, difficult to open, but she wanted to look up into his darkly watchful face.

'How long…?' she managed through the burn of sensuality that was flooding every part of her. 'How long can this last?'

'Until I've had enough. Until I'm sated with you— or you with me. We might have six months, we might have a year, but I promise you in all the time we are together I'll never look at another woman, never give you cause to be jealous. And when it's over I'll tell you straight. No pretence. No lies.'

'Total honesty,' Emily murmured. She could take that.

'Total honesty,' Vito agreed deeply, taking her mouth again.

His hands were where she needed them now. They stroked and smoothed, caressed their way over the skin exposed by the short sleeves of her dress, slipped in at the scooped neckline, branding heat and need on the sensitive flesh. Her breasts felt tight and swollen, aching for his touch on their sensitivity, pressing themselves against the hard wall of his chest as he crushed her to him.

'Emilia, tesoro...'

It was a low, rough mutter deep in his throat as he caught her hair in long, powerful fingers, pulling her head back so that he could take her mouth again, white teeth tugging softly on the lower lip where just moments before his thumb had smoothed away the evidence of her doing the same. And then a moment later a sweep of his tongue eased the tiny pain.

'I have wanted this—dreamed of this... '

Emily felt as well as heard the words as Vito murmured them against her neck, making her arch back so that she exposed the fine lines, the smooth skin that he kissed his way down, lingering at the base of her throat where her heightened pulse beat rapidly under his caress.

Hard, hot hands found the curves of her breasts, stroking the sides for a moment before cupping them both in his palms and smoothing his thumbs across the swollen, peaking nipples. Her breasts had never felt so thin-skinned, so sensitive in her life before. The sensation was so wild, so fierce that Emily flung her head even further back, arching into him even more, her eyes closing as she savoured the sharp intensity of pleasure that came almost close to pain.

'Vito…'

His name was a moan of delight, of encouragement, of…

'No!'

The sensual pleasure died, replaced rapidly by a shock like cold water splashing into her face as her pleasure-drunk brain suddenly registered the cruel and unwanted shaft of reality that sliced into the heated delirium that had her in its grip.

How could she have forgotten…?

How could she *enjoy* the heightened sensitivity of her breasts when the reason for that was one that passion had burned from her mind? But now a tiny, fearful, rational voice was screaming at her from the darkness on the sides of the red haze of sensuality that was melting her brain.

Her breasts were so newly sensitive because she was expecting a baby—his baby—and in a moment if this continued then Vito was going to find out…

'No…' she tried again but he didn't hear or if he did then he wasn't listening because his proud dark head had left her throat and moved lower, lower, kissing his way over one breast, that tormenting mouth heading for the hard, tight nipple that pushed so proudly against the fine material of her dress.

'N—' Emily began again, only to have the sound choke off in her throat, turning into a wild moan of delight as Vito's tongue swirled over her breast, moistening the cotton that covered her before letting his mouth close over her nipple and suckling hard.

'Oh, no!'

That might have been what she wanted to say, but the sound came out as nothing like the command to stop she meant it. Or did she truly want it to be that way? Didn't she really want to express herself the way it was as a cry of such sensual satisfaction that it encouraged him to even more caresses, even more sensual torment?

She knew she should stop him, had to stop him.

But the truth was that she *couldn't* stop him. Not when the only way was to clutch at his dark head with her hands and pull it upwards by the hair, dragging him away from her. But her hungry body wouldn't let her act on what she knew she had to do. And her fearful mind dodged away from the inevitable repercussions of her actions if she did.

So she could only linger as she was, half in delight, half in an agony of fearful apprehension. She was unable to fully enjoy the sensual touch, the stinging kisses and yet she couldn't bear to make them stop, couldn't tear herself away from his arousing embrace, even though it might lead to discovery. Inevitable disaster when he found…

Her mind froze in pure icy panic as those knowing hands slid lower, stroking over her hips, down her thighs. When warm, hard fingers moved under her dress, lifting the loose skirt, and trailed burning, erotic patterns up the tender skin they found there she froze into panicked stillness, knowing that to stop him now, to reach down and drag his hand away, would be as dangerous as to stand outside in the wildest thunderstorm, shielding herself only in metal and defying the lightning strikes to do their worst. Moving away would only rouse his suspicions, make him think her a cold-blooded tease .

But oh, which was worse—to be thought a tease or *this?* How could she let him find out this way— and yet how could she *tell* him now…?

'Vito—Vito…'

His name was a whispered refrain on painfully dry lips, her heart racing so high up in her throat that it was making it impossible to breathe, and all the while she knew that he must believe her reaction to be one of delight. Of pleasure, when the terrible truth was…

No—she had to stop this—had to tell him…

'Vito…' she tried desperately. 'Vito, please, I have something…'

But it was already too late. Those knowing hands had reached the feminine centre of her body, sliding over the cotton and lace of her underwear, cupping her most intimate flesh and then—and then…

He froze. With his hands still on her, still curved on the gentle swell of her belly, the unmistakable sign, only small as yet to the eye perhaps, but oh, so obvious to the touch—the curve of her flesh beneath which slept her baby—his baby…

'You're pregnant!'

She'd expected a roar of fury and had been nerving herself to see the dark blaze of anger in his eyes. Instead she found that she was face to face with an iceman. With a man whose features had become immobile, his jaw set tight, his mouth a slashing line across his face. Only his eyes seemed alive and they burned like black ice, searing across her skin like a blade.

But it was his voice that froze her own blood in her veins, stilling her breath and making it impossible to move or think, or even react in any way.

'You are pregnant,' he said again, each syllable cold and clear, as if carved from the ice that formed his eyes. '*Lei é incinta,*' he repeated as if only stating the fact in his native language could bring the fact home to him.

His ice-dark eyes held her transfixed, as if the cold from them had imprisoned her in the one spot, unable to move. His long, tense body radiated hostility and barely controlled fury, but none of it showed in his face or in his voice. He was so totally, ruthlessly under control that it made her shiver in her shoes, her legs feeling like water beneath her.

And all the time his hands still curved across her belly in a mockery of the gentle, loving caress that a brand-new father might give his child while it was still in the womb. A caress that included the beloved mother of his child in the same tender moment.

But she was not the beloved mother of his child. And if he had had his way she should not have been carrying a child at all.

And—

'Madre de Dio...'

Her thoughts splintered as Vito's savage curse shattered the terrible stillness in the air. Snatching his hands away as if he had been burned, he swung away from her, the force of his movement expressing the violence of his thoughts as he went first to the window to stare out across the wide expanse of the lawn, then turned back again and paced from one end of the room to the other and back again.

'Vito...' Emily quavered but if her voice reached him he ignored it and kept up the restless, furious pacing, pacing like a caged lion, as if he couldn't bear or cope with being still.

At the far end of the room he paused again, staring out of a different window, at a different view, and the stiff, taut length of his back, the aggressive set of the broad shoulders might have been a high stone wall complete with cruel barbed wire set along the top, they expressed so firmly the hard and unyielding command, 'Keep out! *Keep out!*'

Vaguely, in the back of her mind, Emily registered a sound from the front of the house. The sound of tyres on gravel as a car approached. But she couldn't let it distract her, didn't dare to focus her attention on that instead of—

'Vito…' she tried again but even as she was still speaking he had rounded on her again and she knew the question he was going to ask before he even opened his mouth.

'You said you were on the Pill…' He flung the accusation in her face and even from the distance of several feet she felt the lash of his tongue like the flick of a cruel whip.

'I know I did—but—' she tried but he dismissed the stumbling attempt at explanation with another of those brutal, slashing movements of his hand, cutting her off in mid sentence. There was something he needed to know much more urgently than that.

'The child,' he said, his voice rough and harsh. 'This baby—is it mine?'

'I…' Emily was still struggling with the first question, trying to get her bruised and battered mind to think straight, to explain what had happened in the most acceptable way. The way that might just lessen the bitter fury that had him in its grip or at least ease his mood enough to make him listen.

'You see…'

'No, I don't see! I don't see anything at all! You said you were on the Pill—you promised me that you were protected and yet…'

'Yes.' It was all that Emily could manage, her voice low and miserable, her gaze fixed on the floor, unable to meet the black, glittering coldness of his beautiful eyes. 'Yes, I know.'

Outside a car door slammed and footsteps headed towards the front door. She knew who it was, of course. At precisely the worst possible moment, Joe McKenzie had finally turned up.

She knew that Vito had heard him too, but not by so much of a flicker in his eyes or a change of expression on his face did he show any reaction. Instead he took a couple of long, angry strides towards her, caught her chin in his hand again and lifted her downbent head until she was forced to look him in the face.

'I want an answer, Emilia,' he told her harshly. 'And I want the truth. The baby that you're carrying: is it mine?'

There was only one answer she could give him. He had demanded the truth and there was nothing else she could say. Swallowing hard and steeling herself to meet that burning gaze, she took a deep, unsteady breath and brought the words out in a rush.

'Yes! Yes, yes, yes—the baby's yours. It's yours—your child, all right? It's *yours!*'

At last the words were out. Her shoulders slumped with the sheer relief of having the truth out in the open, then tensed again at the thought of what might be coming next. How was Vito going to react? What was he going to do?

She had told him that she was on the Pill—promised him that there would be no repercussions from the night of passion they had shared. But events and circumstances had conspired against her so that, unknowing, she had broken that promise and the result of that was there, in her womb, five months later. A baby. A baby that Vito had never wanted. A baby that he had not known existed—until now.

And now that he knew…

'Mine,' Vito said in a tone and with an expression that she found impossible to interpret.

And before she could begin to do so, the footsteps outside came right up to the door and the next moment the sound of the bell rang through the room.

CHAPTER ELEVEN

YES—the baby's yours. It's yours—your child.

My child.

The baby that Emily was carrying was his child—a baby he had only just discovered existed. A baby that *she* had known about for five months. Carried for five months.

Kept secret for five months.

And would have continued to keep secret from him if he hadn't turned up here so unexpectedly.

The memory of why he had come here, the thoughts that had been in his mind as he turned the car into the drive, the hunger that had been beating at him from the moment he had first seen her at the window, all paled into insignificance beside this one fact, this one huge, stunning, major fact.

Emily Lawton was pregnant with his child.

She was waiting for his reaction. He looked into her pale face, into her wide, apprehensive blue eyes.

She did right to look apprehensive, damn her!

She had known all this time and then she had let him find out this way...

She hadn't even *told* him! She had let him find out ...

'Vito...' Emily began, her voice weak and uncertain, and he could feel the faint tremor in her chin where he still held it clamped between his finger and thumb. 'Please...'

'No!'

She wanted to talk. Wanted him to say how he felt. He wasn't ready to say anything! How the hell could he *talk* when he didn't even know how he felt—couldn't begin to think about it?

'No.'

He released her, stepped back, holding up his hands like a barrier between them.

'No.'

'But Vito—' she tried again, breaking off sharply when the doorbell rang for the second time, interrupting them again. Her blonde head turned sharply, her gaze going towards the door, then back to his face again.

'That's Joe...' she said hesitantly. 'The estate agent. He knows I'm expecting him.'

'Answer it.' He growled the command, knowing he could do nothing else.

'But—'

'Answer it!' And then, as the bell rang yet again. 'Open the door now. He isn't going to go away. Go!'

He gave her a slight push when she still hesitated.

Watching her hurry to the door, straightening her hair, her dress, as she went was a form of torture when his body was still aching in arousal, still hungry for the sensual satisfaction that he had clamped down on so suddenly and so shockingly. The sway of her hips was pure temptation but he wasn't going to let himself even think about that. With the return of a degree of control came a return of more rational thought.

And rational thought shone a very different light on things.

The baby's yours...your child.

She'd sounded genuine enough, but then so had Loretta. Loretta had claimed to be carrying his child so as to trap him into marriage. And she'd damn nearly succeeded.

That was not going to happen again.

But one thing was sure. There was a child. And quite clearly a child that had been conceived some months ago.

Five months? He'd need confirmation of that.

'So where would you like to start?'

Emily had come back into the room with a small, stout, balding man who carried a clipboard and a large measuring tape. The pink flush that had washed her cheeks still hadn't totally faded, giving her more colour than she'd had since he'd arrived.

'Oh—and Joe, this is…' she hesitated over the name, the blood racing into her skin once again '…Signor Corsentino. He's—he's just leaving.'

She accompanied the words with a blatant glare and a swift, signalling glance towards the door. A signal that Vito was determined to ignore.

'There's been a change of plan about that,' he drawled, stepping past her to shake the estate agent's hand. 'I thought it better if I stayed.'

If she believed that he was going to back out quietly after the news she'd just given him and give her a chance to regroup and recover then she had better think again. Once this estate agent's visit was over they had some talking to do—and he wanted some very good answers.

Besides, there was something about this situation that set his teeth on edge. There were undercurrents that swirled around Emily and the fact that she was selling the house—problems that he meant to get to the bottom of. And soon.

So he accompanied Emily and Joe McKenzie as

they went from room to room, observing every-thing as he went and taking in as much as he could from them.

It was a big house, large, and elegant. But it had obviously seen better days and there were places where the neglect was more than just letting the decoration grow shabby, or the curtains fade.

So was this why she was selling up? Had her husband perhaps not left her enough money to maintain even the standard of living that they had once enjoyed? Or was she planning on a very dif-ferent way of life from this quiet, countryside existence?

One thing that intrigued him was the complete lack of any photographs of Emily or her husband. Most homes had at least one or two—a wedding photograph if nothing else—but he couldn't spot a single one on his journey round the house. It was almost as if she had erased the man she had married from her life. There wasn't even one in the small single bedroom that unexpectedly turned out to be where Emily herself slept; the only room with any personal items in it at all. And that room too was a surprise. Why, when she could have had her pick of the four big double bedrooms, particu-larly the one that overlooked the large garden at the back, would she have chosen this small, shabby room that didn't even have an *en suite* bathroom?

He added the question to the list of those he wanted answering when he was alone with Emily once again.

They were going to have one hell of a lot to talk about.

'So that's everything, I think.'

Emily focused her attention totally on Joe McKenzie and tried hard to keep her voice calm and neutral. It was the only way she could keep a grip on the unsettling, uncomfortable emotions that had been swirling through her ever since Vito had arrived at the house. In the space of less than half an hour she felt as if she had been on a wild roller-coaster ride, shooting up and down until her head spun and she was dizzy and sick with stress. So that now she could barely see straight and it was an effort just to keep putting one foot in front of the other while keeping herself upright.

'Perhaps you'd like to come back downstairs and have a drink while we discuss the details.'

She wasn't going to look at Vito, wasn't even going to acknowledge his existence as she led the way down the big curving staircase into the hall and through into the living room. All through the lengthy inspection of the house that had once been her home, she had been painfully, uneasily aware of his dark, silent presence, always there, just at her right shoulder so that if she turned her head she saw his big, powerful form prowling along beside her like some lean, muscled hunting cat. Those deep grey eyes had looked everywhere, seen everything, noted everything. So many times she had glanced at his face to see the way they were narrowed in sharp assessment, fierce as a laser, and she could almost hear that cool, incisive brain working inside his head, taking in everything—and coming to what sort of conclusions?

She wished she knew what he was thinking. Wished that she didn't have to do this in front of him; that she didn't have to wash some of her dirty linen in front of him. Because she had very little hope that she was going to be able to get away without doing just that.

But she was going to try. Vito was still following when they reached the living room and so, as Joe McKenzie had seated himself and started making notes on the paper on his clipboard, Emily turned deliberately in the doorway, blocking off the other man's entry to the room.

'Didn't you say you had to leave about now?' she asked pointedly, directing a small, tight, fake-polite smile up into his face. A smile that was purely for Joe McKenzie's benefit and which had no real warmth or softness in it at all.

'I think not.'

Vito's smile was as meaningless as hers had been but there was something behind it, something dark and faintly dangerous, that made her shiver in spite of the warmth of the morning sun. Don't challenge me on this, was the warning that threaded through his words, giving them an ominous edge that stripped away the apparently easy tone and left it stark and brutal, totally un-compromising in a way that only Emily was aware of. To Joe, who couldn't see those deep dark eyes, the obdurate set of the strong jaw, it was simply polite conversation.

'We have things we still need to talk about…'

Cold grey eyes dropped to her belly to make it only too plain just what those 'things' were, then came up again to clash with her own gaze in a silent battle in which there could only ever be one winner.

'But they can wait until you've finished your business with Mr McKenzie,' Vito went on with a change of tone that made Emily blink in shaken astonishment.

If she hadn't seen that deliberate, provocative movement of his eyes, seen the way that his sensual mouth had thinned in barely controlled irritation, she would never have suspected there was anything but easy-going consideration in Vito's behaviour. And she was still staring in bewilderment when he put his hands on her shoulders and spun her round, walking her into the room and towards one of the chairs.

'So why don't I make more coffee while you concentrate on that?'

I don't want coffee and if I did I most definitely wouldn't want *you* to make it! Emily wanted to shout after him as he strolled towards the kitchen, where she had made him a drink almost an hour before.

But of course she couldn't, not with an audience. She knew only too well that Joe McKenzie would be going straight from here to Mark's family, and the news of a stand-up fight between her sister-in-law and a mysterious, handsome Italian would be just the sort of gossip that Ruth would latch on to with greed, wanting to know everything about it.

So she forced herself to sit down with Joe and

tried to concentrate on what he was saying about the condition of the house and the state of the market. Not that any of it really mattered to her. She didn't have a hope in hell of finding the money to buy any sort of house, let alone find the cost of this particular enormous place. And when Joe finally came up with his valuation, the amount he named made her blink hard in shock.

'So that's the price I'll be putting on the house,' he said. 'I'm sure Mrs Hastings will find it satisfactory.'

'I'm sure Ruth will,' Emily managed, her voice breaking slightly as she struggled to absorb the full implications of the enormous cost. 'She's never liked this place anyway and she'd much rather have the money.'

'But where will you live?' Joe's concern showed in his hazel eyes.

'Wherever I can find.'

Emily sighed. Casting a quick glance towards the kitchen, where the sound of cups and saucers being placed on the worktop showed that Vito was absorbed and out of earshot, she went on, 'And, considering what you've just told me about the housing market, that's not going to be easy.'

'Not without substantial funds behind you. I

must say, my dear that I really couldn't believe it when I heard what Mark had done.'

Joe shook his head in disapproval and disbelief.

'It really shouldn't have been that way.'

'It's all water under the bridge now, Joe.'

Emily tried a smile but her lips felt as if they were stretched too tight. As if they might actually crack or splinter if she tried to put any real emotion behind it.

'And to be honest, I'd really rather have it this way. So tell me, when this place goes on the market, how long do you think I'll have—before I have to think about moving out? Will it be easy for Ruth to get a buyer, do you think?'

Joe looked dubious just at the thought of re-sponding to her question and that gave Emily her answer without him having to speak. So it wasn't any sort of a shock, but still the news was worse than she had thought.

'Last house like this I had on the books, someone snapped it up within the week.'

'A week!'

Emily's spirits, already low, plummeted right to the soles of her feet. She had hoped for a little more time to prepare and this was worse than even her very worst fears. Instinctually her hand went to her body curving protectively over the spot where her baby lay.

'At that price!'

What was she going to do? Where was she going to go? It was no good turning to Ruth. Her sister-in-law had considered that she was being generous enough letting her stay on until now. She wouldn't hesitate to throw her out just as soon as the house sold.

'It's a bargain, you see—not been kept up to scratch; needing renovations. People like that sort of thing and—'

'Coffee?'

The question came from behind them, making Emily start nervously. When had Vito come out of the kitchen, and how much had he heard? Just the thought made her hand shake as she turned to reach up for the cup.

'That is for Signor McKenzie,' Vito told her. 'I brought water for you.'

'I can make up my own mind about what I drink!' Emily protested, furious at the way he had made the decision for her.

'You want to be ill?'

The brilliant grey eyes challenged her coldly, daring her to question his authority.

'I saw how you were earlier. A coffee won't suit you any better now. However if you want to be sick…'

He held the coffee-cup out towards her.

If anything was guaranteed to make her concede, that was it. She might try for bravado to make sure that he didn't trample all over her but actually drinking coffee was quite beyond her. Just the thought of it made her feel decidedly queasy. But she played the game a moment or two longer, taking the cup deliberately before turning to pass it on to Joe and accept the glass of water instead.

A moment later she was intensely grateful she had because nothing could stop a jolting reaction of total shock that would have sent hot coffee flying everywhere when Vito came and sat beside her on the settee and, placing his own cup securely on the table in front of him, asked in a voice so calm and matter-of-fact that he might have been wanting to know the price of bread, 'So will your client accept a private arrangement, Signor McKenzie?'

'*What?*'

Not believing what she had heard, Emily turned to face him, anxious eyes searching his face to see just what he was talking about, because he couldn't

mean what she thought he did—he just couldn't.
But Vito totally ignored her shock and bewilderment, concentrating instead on Joe McKenzie, directing all his attention to the other man.

'I'll pay the asking price—include your commission as well—but only if we agree on the deal
now, and the house doesn't even go on the market.'

'Vito!' Emily tried to protest, tried to intervene.
This couldn't be real—it wasn't happening.

But Vito simply held up one hand in a gesture
to silence her, not even looking in her direction,
but keeping his dark-eyed gaze fixed on the man
before him.

'Do we have a deal?'

'You want to buy this house?'

Joe looked every bit as dumbfounded as Emily
felt, his expression growing even more bewildered
as Vito inclined his dark head in agreement.

'That's exactly what I want. But only on those
terms.'

'But—can I ask why?'

Vito shrugged a negligent dismissal of the
question as unimportant.

'I need a base in England. I came on the inspection of the house with you—and I liked what I
saw. I think this house will suit me perfectly.'

'It's a big house for a single man …'

'Ah, but I'm planning on getting married soon.'

Married. The word sounded like a death knell inside Emily's head and it was only when it did that she admitted to herself that somewhere deep inside there had been some tiny, silly, stupid little bit of her that had actually hoped…

She had let herself dream that Vito had meant it when he had said, 'I came for you.' She'd even allowed herself to be seduced, enticed by the flattering declaration that he hadn't been able to get her out of his mind and so he wanted—needed—to spend more time with her. The lying, cheating declaration that had just been deliberately aimed at one thing and one thing only—getting her back into his bed.

And the two-faced bastard was getting married!

'You…!' she began but the fierce, burning-eyed glare that Vito flung in her direction silenced her in a split-second and he turned his attention back to the stunned-looking estate agent.

'Well?'

'Well—yes, I'm sure that Mrs Hastings will agree. She's looking for a quick sale and this must be one of the quickest on record. But—er—don't you think that perhaps you should be asking someone else before you make the final decision? Wouldn't your fiancée like to have a say in this? Wouldn't it be better if you let her see the place first?'

'She's already seen it,' Vito stated calmly, startling Emily so much that the glass of water jerked in her hand, spilling some of the liquid over the sides.

'She loves the house. But if you'd like me to make sure, I will. Emily…'

For the first time since he had come to sit down he turned towards her fully, angling his long body so that he was facing her, looking into her stunned and bewildered eyes.

'Would you like to continue to live here?'

Now what was he doing? Was he deliberately setting out to twist the knife that he had so brutally stabbed into her already wounded heart? Not content with announcing that he was getting married and that he wanted to buy the house—her home—for himself and his fiancée, now he had the cruel nerve to ask …

'Don't do this to me! How can you even ask me such a question? You know I would but…'

'*Molto bene.*'

Vito actually reached out and patted her hand before turning back to where Joe McKenzie was sitting in stunned silence, watching the interplay between them.

'You see, there is no problem, none at all. My fiancée loves the house as much as I do and she wants to live here too.'

'What?'

Emily couldn't believe what she was hearing. Her brain was totally scrambled and none of this made any sense.

'Vito, what are you—why are you saying that?'

What was he saying? In her confusion, she almost thought that he had told Joe that *she* was his fiancée, but surely that couldn't possibly be right?

'I know, *tesoro...*'

Vito's calm, soothing tone made her blink in disbelief, and the gentle, understanding smile he sent her way only piled more confusion on top of disbelief.

'I know we said that we would keep our coming marriage secret for a time but when you want this house so much and Signor McKenzie is in a position to arrange the deal for us, I knew you wouldn't mind.'

'But...' Emily spluttered but Vito swept on, ignoring her attempt to protest.

'So I can leave that with you, *signor*?'

He was standing up, shaking hands with Joe, ushering him towards the door, and Emily could only watch them go, fake a smile and try to get her mind back into focus.

She couldn't start an argument now, not when Joe was clearly already intrigued enough. It was obvious that he was as keen as could be to get out and report back to Ruth. He had much more of a story than he had ever dreamed he'd have to tell. So she wasn't going to risk saying anything more in front of him. Ruth would just love to think that the supposed engagement was already in trouble—maybe even over before it had started. That thought gagged her as successfully as if Vito had actually bound a cloth right over her mouth.

So she couldn't say anything now. But she only had to wait a few minutes and then she was going to give the arrogant, domineering, interfering Vito Corsentino several pieces of her mind!

He was coming back, strolling into the room with that devastatingly sexy prowl he had, and he was looking totally smug—well, she was going to enjoy wiping that self-satisfied expression from his handsome face.

Realising that she was still clutching the glass of water, holding it as if it were a weapon, she set it down carefully on the coffee-table. Otherwise, the temptation to throw the glass or at least its contents right in Vito's face might just prove too much for her. Then she stood up—she needed to be able to look him right in the face for this—and waited until he was close enough for her to see the gleam of satisfaction deep in those dark eyes.

But not for long.

'So what the hell do you think you're playing at?'

That got his attention. He blinked hard, just once, and to her delight she saw the glint of amusement leave his gaze. Instead, the look he turned on her was pure, wicked innocence, so guileless and open that she almost felt she could imagine him in a choirboy's cassock and ruff.

But she also knew that the look was a total fake, carefully assumed just for her benefit.

'Playing, *carissima?*' he questioned. 'I don't believe I know what you mean. There is no game.'

'Oh, come off it! Don't try and use the "I am but a poor, simple Italian—I do not understand your language" card!' Emily scoffed. 'You speak English almost as well as I do and you know very well what I mean.'

The smile lingered but something had changed in his eyes. The light faded fast, leaving them bleak and cold in a way that drained all the warmth from his smile, made it hard and distant, sending a sensation of something nasty and uncomfortable sliding down her spine.

'I understand the English,' he stated, clipped and crisp, even the lyrical accent almost totally erased, 'but I do not see the reason for it.'

'You don't think that I might object to you moving in and taking over my life, dictating what is going to happen and when?'

'And when did I do that?'

'When?'

Emily threw up her hands in exasperation, sparing a moment to be grateful for the fact that she no longer held the water glass. The contents would have gone everywhere if she did.

'Do you have to ask? Just here, just now—you barged in and...'

'I bought you a house.'

Did Vito really not understand what she was trying to say or did he not comprehend the reasons why she objected? It had to be one or the other that had turned those stunning features into the taut, intimidating mask that made her feel as if every word she said had slammed hard against a brutal iron barrier, making it impossible to reach him.

'And this is a problem—why?'

'You didn't *just* buy me a house!' Emily ex-claimed, knowing that as she spoke the words she could understand something of his hostility.

Declared out loud like this, it sounded impossibly petty and ungrateful to be throwing his gift back in his face. But the problem was that it was not just the gift—it was everything else that came with it.

'You set out to take over my life—buying this house for me when I didn't ask you to, dictating ev-erything I should do…telling Joe we're engaged, for God's sake… You must know that he'll go and tell Ruth everything you said just now. And then when it all turns out to be a pretence—'

'But it will not.'

'Of course it will—it has to…we're not getting married!'

'Oh, but we are.'

If it had been said with any sort of bravado, or a touch of anger, or even the tiniest hint of triumph then Emily would never have believed Vito's answer. But the reality was that it was stated in such a calm, flat, matter-of-fact way that it hit home like a bullet to her heart, leaving her staring with shocked, unfocused eyes, gasping for breath as she struggled to accept what she had heard.

'Don't be crazy, Vito,' she managed in a voice that had no strength to it at all. 'And please stop playing games. Give me one good reason why we're likely to get married when we don't even like, let alone love each other.'

Those broad shoulders under the pale blue shirt shrugged off her comment with insulting carelessness.

'Love doesn't come into this,' he stated coldly, taking several steps forward until he was standing directly opposite her, looking down into her indignant, hostile face. 'We don't come into it— except as the ones who have to take responsibility for our actions.'

And then, of course she knew where he was going with this. She'd known it from the start, just hadn't wanted to admit it to herself. He was going to say that they must marry for the baby and only for the baby.

And she knew that she couldn't bear to let that happen. She didn't dare to ask herself why it must not happen. She only knew that it couldn't.

Desperation clawed at her thoughts, ripping through the thick fog that clouded them, letting in a tiny speck of light, showing her a path she could take.

Of course. She should have thought of that sooner. It should have been so obvious, so undeniable. But just the idea of Vito claiming her as his fiancée had fused so many circuits in her brain that she hadn't been able to see what was right before her face.

She snatched at the answer in the way that a drowning man would grab at any piece of flotsam that drifted by. It was a way out and she had to take it even though the sudden bitter wrench of her heart as she formed the words in her mind almost made her hesitate, almost drained all her courage from her.

'Vito, don't do this! You know it isn't going to work—that it's totally impossible. Even if I wanted to marry you—what good would it do? You know very well that you couldn't possibly afford this house.'

She knew her point had struck home when she saw his face change again. Even the cold light that had been in his eyes died, and his mouth clamped into a thin, hard line.

'And that matters to you, does it?'

'It matters because you've just told the estate agent that you'll buy this house—and pay him his commission. He might have swallowed your story and gone away dreaming of the fastest sale he's

ever had in his life, the easiest income he's ever
earned, but you forget I've seen your flat and the
way you live. You don't have a hope of buying a
place like this.'

What had she said now, to change his expression
yet again? What had she said that brought a hint
of a smile back to his mouth, but a smile that was
made from pure ice, no trace of warmth in it at all?

'You'd like to think that, wouldn't you, *mia
angela?* But I'm afraid that I'm going to have to
disillusion you. You see, you have it all wrong. You
saw the way I was living and naturally you
assumed that it was the way I always lived—but
that is not so.'

That worrying smile grew, became cruel,
hateful. It was the smile that might have been on
the face of a hunting cat just before it leapt to tear
its small, frightened prey into tiny pieces.

'No?'

It was just a voiceless croak. Try as she might,
she couldn't make a sound; her throat was too
parched, her lips painfully dry. Nervously Emily
slicked her tongue over them to ease the discomfort and tried again.

'No?'

This time it worked. But she wished that she

hadn't spoken when she saw the cold burn of his eyes, the faint flare of something that made her shiver in apprehension.

'No, *tesoro,*' he murmured, lacing the words with deadly softness. 'No, it's not the truth at all. *Al contrario*—the reality is that if I wanted I could buy this house—and you—a hundred times over.'

CHAPTER TWELVE

HE'D known that the truth had to come out some time, Vito admitted to himself. There was no way that Emily could continue to believe that the small flat he'd been living in when they had met was really the way he lived—the only lifestyle he knew. But if he was honest then he would have preferred it not to have been like this.

The timing was really not the best. Just when he had thought that things were going the way he wanted them, the realisation that the Vito Corsentino she had met five months before was not the real Vito Corsentino had caused Emily to slam the brakes on hard. But he did at least owe her an explanation.

'Perhaps we should sit down,' he said, gesturing towards the settee.

'Why—will I need to?' Emily enquired tartly, making him draw in his breath in an exasperated hiss and rake both hands forcefully through his hair. She was as prickly as a hedgehog, determined not to yield an inch.

'I just thought you'd prefer to be comfortable. You need to take care of yourself.'

The glare she flung at him said without words she had been looking after herself for five months, without him! But surprisingly she conceded to do as he said—though he noticed that she chose one of the big armchairs and not the settee so that he couldn't go and sit beside her.

But sitting opposite, on the arm of the other armchair, he could see right into her face, watch every expression that slid across her features, hope to read what was going through her mind.

'I was taking time out when we met.'

Those blue eyes slanted him a distinctly suspicious look. One that said he was going to have to work hard at this if he was going to convince her.

'Time out from what?'

'From the business that Guido—my brother—and I run.'

'Guido—the man who came to Amber's wedding?'

'Yes.'

It was as Vito nodded in response to the wary question that he remembered what his brother had told him about his meeting with Emily at that wedding. She had fainted, Guido had said. Collapsed so badly that she had fallen onto the floor from the pew in which she'd been sitting. And then later, at the hotel where the reception should have been held, she'd accosted him, calling by his brother's name. Calling him Vito. He'd known she was lying when she'd claimed she hadn't thought about him once in the five months they'd been apart, but still the recollection of what Guido had told him about her reaction made him pause to consider.

'So what is this business? It's big, I presume?'

He saw her eyes flick towards the window and knew she was thinking about the sleek, expensive car parked outside the house.

'Big enough. Guido and I built up Corsentino Marine from nothing. Years ago, when we first started out on trying to rebuild the company's fortunes, Guido and I made a promise to each other. We were working twenty-four hours every day that God sent. We never had holidays, never had days off. So we swore an oath—if we suc-ceeded as we dreamed, before we were thirty, then for both of us our thirtieth year would be free—to do with as we pleased. To stop being

Corsentino of Corsentino Marine—and, later, Corsentino Leisure—and just be ourselves— Guido and Vito. Living where we wanted and doing what we wanted while the other one ran the business on his own.'

Those blue eyes that were fixed on him had widened. This was not what she expected; it was written all over her pretty face.

'You could afford to do that?'

'We could both afford never to work again if we wanted. Guido's a year older than I am so he had his break year first. He went to America; spent a year there as a photographer.'

And had come home with a broken heart, he recalled, allowing himself a small, secret smile at the way that Guido's life had worked out since.

'That was when he met your friend Amber. The first time. Before he appeared at her wedding last week.'

'She's not exactly a friend of mine. The man she was supposed to have married, Rafe St Clair, was a friend of Ma—of my husband.'

Something about the way she said the other man's name caught on Vito's nerves.

'You didn't like him? St Clair, I mean?'

'I didn't trust him. And to be honest—no, wait

a minute, you're trying to distract me from the fact that you lied to me.'

'Not lied. Be honest, you didn't exactly ask any questions. Neither did I.'

His tone darkened as he remembered the way he felt when he had realised that he *should* have asked those questions. He could still taste the bitterness that disillusionment had left in his mouth. And by the way that hot colour washed Emily's cheeks, she was thinking much the same thoughts.

'So your brother spent his year being a photographer. And I take it that this year it was your turn and you wanted to spend some time in England? What did you want to do?'

'Carving.'

'Carving? You mean in wood?'

'Exactly. My family were boat builders by trade. In the past they would have got their hands dirty— done the job themselves. I expect that the love of wood and making things in it was passed down to me from my ancestors. That was why I had the flat by the shore. I would collect driftwood and see what it said to me. See what shape or animal was inside it.'

'Those wooden creatures in your flat—they were your work?'

'They were.'

'But they were wonderful—beautiful.'

'Grazie.'

Did she know what it did to her face when it lit up that way in enthusiasm? The way that her eyes seemed to glow, and a wash of colour flooded her cheeks? The curve of her mouth begged for his kisses and that smile could have brightened the darkest night.

The hard, hot kick of sexual hunger that hit at him made him wince inwardly. And yet somehow this time it was so very different. He had come here today to get that physical need out of his system, but he'd been stopped dead in his tracks by the realisation that Emily was pregnant. There was no way now that he was going to be able to sate himself on her and walk away. So what did he put in its place?

Marriage seemed the obvious answer. With a baby on the way, the only answer. So what the hell was she doing being so damn stubborn about the idea?

Unless she had good reason not to marry him.

What if the baby wasn't his after all? He'd believed her—but women lied about these things. Loretta was proof of that.

'So now that you know the truth about me— does that make things easier for you?'

'Easier?'

Emily couldn't understand where that comment had come from. What could Vito possibly mean? And how could knowing more about him make anything in this appalling situation any easier?

'Make what easier?'

'I would have thought that this made it a lot easier for you to accept my proposal of marriage.'

'In what way?'

'Well, now you know that I can keep you in— what is it?—the manner in which you would like to live. I would have thought that that—'

'You actually think that just because you turn out to be wealthy I'll be happy to marry you?'

Emily couldn't believe what she was hearing. Did he really believe that the only possible reason she might have for wanting to be with him was for his money? From the cold light in his eyes, it was obvious that that was what was in his mind. So had he thought that he could bribe her to marry him by buying the house? Did he think she was nothing more than a gold-digger who would be swayed by what he could give her rather than what he was?

'I don't recall you actually *proposing*. It was more of a unilateral declaration. "I want to buy this house because I'm getting married. Oh, and by the way, Emily is my fiancée!" Tell me, Vito, just where was the question in all that?'

'I don't need to ask. You are carrying my child.'

'And that gives you the right to my life?'

'Maybe not your life—but it does give me rights.'

Reaching out both hands, he placed them on her stomach, curving over the spot where her baby lay. And as he did so his black-eyed gaze held hers, fiercely mesmeric, impossible to pull away from. His dark expression was totally ruthless, totally in control.

'Do you swear that the baby is mine? A woman lied to me once—I'll not let that happen again.'

Emily swallowed hard, fighting for calm. If she could have, she might have tried to deny it. Tried to tell him that there was a chance it was not his. But when he had added that second comment, she knew there was no way to answer it but:

'Yes. I know that this baby is yours.'

'But you told me you were on the Pill.' Deep-set eyes challenged her, suspicion burning in their depths.

'I was—I *promise* you I was—but events

messed everything up. I left the tablets in my car the night I was with you and the next morning I was in such a hurry to get home that I forgot all about it. That night—things happened to drive it right out of my mind.'

Mark had been taken so much worse. It had been the beginning of the end.

'By the time I got back to my routine it was already too late. I'd missed a couple of days, at just the wrong time.'

'And you *know* that no one else could be the father?'

Emily's heart twisted painfully. She knew where he was heading with this but she didn't dare to acknowledge it for fear something might show in her face that he could interpret the wrong way.

'Who else's could it be?'

'Your husband's?'

Did he really think she would go from his bed to Mark's—or vice versa—without a second thought? If he knew the truth… But, knowing how much he distrusted her, how he thought she was only aiming for the money she'd just learned he had, she only dared to go part of the way into the truth.

'That just wasn't possible!'

'And how can you be so sure?' The challenge was back in his eyes, sweeping over her in burning disdain.

'I know it as a fact. You see…' her voice was very low '…my husband wasn't interested in me that way any more.'

She thought that would reassure him, that it would make him feel better, let him know that he had no room for doubt. That this baby was his and could only be his, no one else's.

But her words seemed to have the opposite effect. She watched even the challenging light fade from his eyes, leaving nothing but black, icy cold. He turned away from her, slowly, every movement seeming to have that exaggerated care of a slow-motion film. And then, just as unhurriedly, he swung back again. But while his movements might have given the impression of being almost lazy and relaxed there was nothing tranquil at all about the expression on his face. His mouth was clamped tight into a thin, hard line, his jaw taut with rigid control, and his eyes just black, gleaming flints behind hooded lids.

'So tell me, *tesoro*…'

The silky drawl was dangerously deceptive,

hiding a barely reined-in savagery behind the smoothness of his tone.

'If your husband hadn't died, would you ever have told me? Or was that what it was all about, hmm?'

'All what was about? I don't know what you're talking about?'

Emily could only stare into his closed, shuttered face in blank confusion. Vito had demanded to know who was the father of the baby she was carrying. He had wanted her to swear to it—to provide proof if she could. And she had done that. She had expected that it would lead him to relax a little at least. That it would make him feel that there was no possibility that she was trying to pass off some other man's child as his own.

Instead she seemed to have alienated him even further, driving him to take many steps back and away from her, both physically and emotionally, and instead of understanding, dark flames of something close to hatred flared in his eyes as he glared at her.

'Was the idea that you'd get yourself pregnant with some other fool's baby—one you could pass off as belonging to your husband and so claim it was his heir? Then you could stay in the house, live in the manner to which you had become accustomed—'

'If that was the plan then it failed miserably! You're forgetting that I can't live here, that I haven't inherited anything—it was all left to my sister-in-law and she's selling the house out from under me!'

'Selling it to me," Vito reminded her coldly. 'So you see, *belleza,* it looks as if you struck lucky after all. I know you love this place—it was obvious from the way you talked about it, the way you looked at each room, touched the walls, the banisters, looked out the windows as you showed the *agente immobiliare* around. You would love to continue to live here.'

'Not at any cost!' Emily tried to interject but Vito ignored her and carried on, his words fuelled by the coldly burning anger that was eating away at his heart.

'You used me to get pregnant with a baby that you believed would ensure you could continue to live in this house, even after your husband was dead. Well, congratulations, *mia angela*—you succeeded better than you ever hoped. Not only do you get the home of your dreams, but you also get a wealthy husband who just happens to be the biological father of your child and who will keep you in luxury for as long as you live.'

'But I said I didn't want to marry you! You don't want to marry me either. Surely we can work out—'

'That part isn't negotiable,' Vito stated adamantly. 'This isn't about you or me but our baby; the new life we have made between us. I want to be in my child's life and so you are going to be my wife and I will be your husband and a father to my child.'

'You can be in your child's life without being my husband! I'll make sure you have access—'

'Access!' Vito scorned, his tone turning the single word into a deadly curse. 'I want to be a full-time father, not just someone with part-time visiting rights.'

'You can't force me to marry you!'

'I won't need to force.'

His voice was low, level, threaded with deadly intent, and as he spoke he came closer, reaching out for her, fastening his hands over the fine bones of her shoulders and drawing her irresistibly closer. She tensed, ready to defend herself, but all he had to do was to loosen his grip, stroke a hand softly over her skin, and within seconds all the fight left her.

She stood there, quivering like some spirited mare that felt the hand of its master, a wild thing, tamed by a firm but gentle hand. Her head came up, blue eyes blazing with defiant rebellion, and her soft mouth trembling faintly. Lowering his head, he let his mouth brush over hers, once, twice, then again, increasing the pressure each time until a low moan escaped her and she let her lips open to his, yielding softly, reluctantly.

'You see, *tesoro*...'

Another kiss drew out a sigh, a soft breath between her lips.

'This is how it will be, when we are married. And will that be such a hardship, hmm?'

Hardship? Emily could only think hazily, drifting on a warm sea of sensuality. How could this be any sort of hardship when he had only to touch her, to kiss her and her soul seemed to fly out of her body and put itself right into his hands? How could she fight what he wanted when it was what she wanted too?

'So—' Vito lifted his dark head and his deep-set eyes burned down into hers, probing right into her thoughts, or so it seemed—'are you determined to fight me on this? Because I warn you if you do then you won't win. I want my child and I mean to have it.'

'You'd—you'd take the baby away from me?' she managed shakily and didn't know whether to feel relief or more fear when he shook his head, the hard set of his jaw not softening in the least.

'I won't need to do that either. Our lives are bound together for the rest of time by this small life we have made between us.'

Once more he laid his hand possessively on the swell of her belly where her baby lay and she felt the child quiver and stir as if it recognised the touch of its father, the presence of a link deeper and more basic than any other possible.

'You will be my wife, and I will take care of both you and my child.'

'You can't just appear on the doorstep and tell me I'm to marry you. I barely know you. We've only known each other for a couple of days! I can't make a decision like that so fast…'

But even as she said it she knew that she was fighting a losing battle, the inevitable was rushing towards her with the ferocity and power of the waves that had swept her off her feet on the day that she had first met Vito on the beach five months before. She was off balance, losing her footing, and very definitely going down for the third time but emotionally rather than physically this time.

Vito lifted his powerful shoulders in a shrug that dismissed her weak-voiced protest as not worth taking the trouble even to consider very seriously.

'Take your time. I'm no brute to drag you to the altar kicking and screaming as I pull you along by your beautiful hair. You can take as long as you need—within reason.'

'Reason?'

Emily struggled to put any force into her protest, feeling every drop of strength fade away from her as if it was seeping out through the soles of her feet and soaking into the carpet where she stood.

'And what's reasonable about any of this? I can take as long as I want—as long as I agree to marry you in the end?'

Vito nodded his dark head, his stunning face set hard as granite, grey eyes opaque with resolution, no hint of any form of yielding in his expression.

'If you want to claim you need time to think—then think. But you will come to the same conclusion in the end—because there is only one conclusion to come to.'

'The conclusion you want!'

'The conclusion that is right,' Vito corrected

248 THE SICILIAN'S RED-HOT REVENGE

with soft but deadly intensity. 'My son or daughter will not be born out of wedlock. That is one thing I am determined on.'

And when Vito Corsentino determined on anything, Emily told herself, struggling against a shiver of fearful reaction, then nothing but nothing got in his way. She was only fooling herself if she thought that she had a chance of holding out against him, but she had at least to try to pretend that she had some fight left in her if only to preserve some degree of self-esteem.

'So take your time, cara, if you need it. Do all the thinking you want. But you know, as do I, that there is nothing to work out except the date and time when our wedding will take place. This is going to happen and there's nothing you can do to stop it.'

CHAPTER THIRTEEN

THE night was dark and silent, the house totally still. Emily should have been asleep hours ago, she had gone to bed as early as she possibly could in order to get away from Vito's oppressive presence, the way that wherever she turned he was always there, watching and waiting, waiting for her answer.

An answer that she couldn't drag up the nerve to give him, even though she knew in her heart that she had no possible alternative. She had spent the last week fighting a bitter, ongoing battle with herself. Fighting against the need to say the words, 'Yes, I'll marry you.' And at the same time fighting her own deep urge to never, ever let herself say just that.

Because the bitter reality was that she could no longer deny the truth to herself. She *wanted* to marry Vito Corsentino. She'd known that almost as soon as he had made his arrogant declaration that she was his fiancée, even though she'd tried to fight against it from the start, telling herself it was the last thing she needed, reminding herself of his cruel words a few short days ago. But the truth was that she'd been deceiving herself all along. Marriage to Vito was something she dreamed of, longed for, wanted with all her heart.

And it was that *heart* that was the trouble.

Lying here in the darkness, with nothing to do but think, she forced herself to face the facts. Somewhere along the line, without knowing how or why it had happened, she had fallen hopelessly, crazily, blindly in love with Vito Corsentino. And as a consequence of that, she longed to marry him: But not like this.

'Not like this!'

The words broke on a sob as she faced the hopelessness of her dreams.

She wanted to marry Vito because he loved her. Because he wanted her so much that he could not live without her. If he loved her then she would have said yes to marriage without a second's hesitation. She would even now be preparing for, looking forward to, the day when she walked down the aisle to marry the man she adored.

But he didn't love her back and because of that she couldn't say yes. She couldn't bear the thought of tying herself for life to a man who only wanted her because she was carrying his child. Who only wanted to make sure that her baby had his name. Who would never love her in the way that she loved him.

Oh, he wanted her all right but that wasn't enough. She'd made one bad mistake that way already, falling into marriage with a man she had believed loved her but who had only ever wanted her in his bed and had almost destroyed her as a result. She had come to hate Mark in the end, ended up desperate to escape from him, and had almost succeeded until a cruel twist of fate had dragged her back into his life again. She couldn't risk that happening with Vito, not even for the hope of some happy years as his wife and the mother of his child.

And so she couldn't possibly say yes to his proposal—his declaration that they should marry.

And yet she couldn't deny him his rightful place in his child's life.

'Oh, Vito…'

His name was just a whisper on her lips, the movement of her mouth making her taste the silent tears that had seeped from her eyes, tears she hadn't even been aware of having shed until then. But once she realised that they were there, then there was nothing she could do but give in to them, abandon herself to the misery that engulfed her. Turning on her side, she buried her face in the pillow and sobbed her heart out.

The sound of the door opening behind her was soft, almost silent, but memories too close to the surface of her thoughts made her ears hypersensitive, catching it, stilling her, then jolting her head up in a rush.

The tall male figure by the door was too much in the shadow for her to see his face. She had only a confused impression of height and strength, a naked chest revealed by the pale light of the moon, dark hair, hidden eyes…

'Mark?'

Vito was heading back to his own room when he heard the barely muffled sobs.

Another night when he couldn't sleep. Another night when lying in his bed thinking of Emily in her bed just down the landing was destroying his peace of mind, eating away at his control. He had vowed to himself that he would wait until she gave him her answer, but he had inflicted the torment of the damned on himself as a result. The only satisfaction that he'd gained from the whole thing was the knowledge that she was as restless as he felt, as the shadows under her eyes in the mornings had borne witness.

Tonight he'd given up on the attempt to sleep and, pulling on a pair of jeans, had gone down to the kitchen to make himself a drink, and it was on his way back to his room that he'd heard the sounds from Emily's bedroom and had gently pushed the door open.

The sound of her sobbing made a cruel hand twist hard in his guts. She was genuinely weeping; sobbing as if her heart would break. And they were not pretty, delicate sobs either, like the ones Loretta had indulged in for careful effect. These were harsh, gulping sobs punctuated by loud, inelegant sniffs. Sobs that made him wince under the attack from his uncomfortable conscience.

The sound of the door opening must have given him away. Emily had heard him and she jolted up from the pillow, turning to stare wide-eyed into the darkness.

'Mark?'

Mark! Vito swore silently and savagely in his native Italian, fighting with the conflicting feelings that assailed him. She had been thinking about her husband, missing him, mourning his loss. The thought made him feel like the lowest sort of rat possible.

'I'm sorry…'

'Vito?'

She was blinking hard now, struggling to focus and swiping the back of her hand at her cheeks to dash away the bitter tears.

'I'm sorry,' he said again, coming to stand closer to the bed. 'I've been a bastard. I never thought—do you miss him very much?'

'Miss…?'

She frowned faintly, twisting until she was sitting upright, with the pillows at her back. Her blonde hair was roughly tousled, the remaining traces of the tear stains still glistening on her cheeks in the moonlight, and one thin strap of the pale pink nightdress she wore had slipped down her arm, revealing the soft creamy curve of her left shoulder. His fingers itched to reach out and smooth it back but he fought the impulse hard.

If he touched her then he would not be able to stop at just that.

'Mark,' he said in answer to her puzzled frown. 'Do you miss your husband…?'

'Miss him…'

The words were punctuated by a hiccup and

another of those sniffs, Emily's voice quavering as her lips trembled, fighting against the control she was clearly struggling to impose. Her neat jaw had tightened, but her shoulders were shaking and those blue eyes, bleached colourless by the moon, swam with more unshed tears.

'Oh, dear God, no! I don't miss him at all.'

Was she laughing or weeping—or some weird combination of the two? Whatever it was, she sounded as if she was about to break, to shatter into tiny pieces.

'But...*Emilia*, what is it?'

That name was the last straw, Emily told herself. The soft, shaken sound of Vito's own private name for her was the thing that finally shattered her precarious grip on her self-control. She couldn't hold back any longer, couldn't keep a grip on the wild combination of tears and laughter that threatened to make her splinter into tiny pieces.

Vito had thought that she was weeping because she missed *Mark*. He had taken the tears that she had shed for *him* to be for the other man instead. She couldn't take it; couldn't cope with the idea. It made her feel as if her heart was actually breaking apart, ripping to pieces inside her chest.

'Oh, Vito...'

The tears were pouring down her cheeks, drenching her skin, and she couldn't see him from behind the curtain of water that blurred her vision. Perhaps that was what finally broke through the restraint she had been imposing on herself, gave her the strength to finally speak, finally admit the truth.

'Vito, you obviously never knew my husband, otherwise you wouldn't even ask such a question. You wouldn't need to…'

'And why is that, *tesoro?*'

Vito had come to sit on the bed, his closeness and the intimate scent of his exposed skin making Emily's heart kick sharply in her chest, and she snatched in an unwary breath as her pulse started to race.

'Why don't you tell me about it? Tell me about Mark—tell me the truth.'

'The—the truth is that Mark—wasn't a man who was easy to love—though I tried—I really tried.'

Her tongue was tangling up in the words, stumbling awkwardly as they fell over one another as she tried to get them out. She had held on to her secrets for so long and now, at last, she wanted the truth out in the open and spoken once and for all.

'I loved him at the start when he asked me to marry him, and I was happy then—just for a while—but then things changed...he changed...'

And now there was no holding back. It was as if the darkness and the stillness of the night had released the lock she had kept on her tongue, pushed her into speech so that everything came tumbling out without plan or order, Emily just letting them fall.

She told of the drinking, the petty tyrannies that had got worse as Mark's alcohol intake had spiralled, the verbal bullying that had swiftly become physical.

'He hit you!' Vito's fury was evident in the way that the words hissed from between clenched teeth, the tight curl of his strong hands into powerful fists on the cream bedcoverings. 'And still you stayed?'

'No!'

Emily shook her head so violently that her blonde hair flew out wildly around her head, soft strands of it brushing against Vito's face, snagging on the late night growth of beard that darkened his chin. Slowly he reached up a hand to ease it away then froze as Emily spoke again.

'No, I didn't stay—I left him. No one would

believe me when I told them what Mark was like, least of all his family. They were sure that I was lying; that I was making it all up. So—so I went. I started divorce proceedings…'

She'd caught the sudden tension in the powerful body next to hers, heard the muttered curse as Vito registered what she'd said.

'I had it all in hand—or thought I had. But then fate stepped in and ruined everything.'

The burn in Vito's dark eyes was almost too much for her. She felt as if it had seared over her skin, scraping off a much-needed protective layer and leaving her shockingly, frighteningly vulnerable. Her own gaze dropped to stare at her hands and so she saw his long bronzed fingers unclench and move, coming to cover hers, curl around them softly.

'What happened?' he asked and his voice was as raw and rough as the feeling in her nerves.

'Mark had been drinking heavily for years. I didn't know it because he'd hidden it from me at first, and even when I knew he drank I didn't know how much. He'd damaged himself terribly—so badly that he had a massive stroke, and then another. He actually died for a few minutes. They managed to bring him round eventually but a part of his brain had been so badly damaged by lack of oxygen that it never recovered.'

Emily drew in a long, low breath and swallowed hard, fighting for the strength to tell the rest of the story. She felt Vito move even closer, felt his arm come round her to support her and leaned back gratefully against its strength.

'The strokes destroyed large chunks of his memory. When he came round he didn't know about the years that had passed—the years we were married. They didn't exist for him. As far as he was concerned, he and I had only just married. We were still in the—in our honeymoon period.'

'And he didn't recall the divorce proceedings?'

Vito didn't need to be told. His voice was as calm and sure as if she'd already told him. Slowly Emily nodded, eyes clouding with more unshed tears.

'He'd never even signed the papers that had been sent to him. I don't know if he saw them.'

'And you went back to him?'

'I had to—he was the Mark I had married. The Mark I'd once loved—and he was so distressed when I wasn't there, it might have killed him. I had to be there with him; to take care of him. But it was wearing—exhausting—and there was never any hope of a cure. The damage to his brain was too severe. But one day I just had to have a break. I had to get away, if only for twenty-four hours.'

'The day we met?'

'The day we met.'

Emily's echoing of his words was low and despondent and one finger traced out the pattern on the bedspread, her eyes fixed on the small movement.

'I chose that day specially.'

Ask me why, she pleaded in the privacy of her thoughts. Please ask me why.

But Vito didn't even need to ask.

'It was the day you had thought you would be divorced. If your husband had been able to sign the papers…'

'Yes.'

Emily's head nodded slowly, her hair brushing against his chest, and she heard his sharp intake of breath at the soft contact with his skin.

'The day I thought I would have—should have had—my freedom. Instead, what I had was a phone call telling me that my husband was asking for me…'

Vito's breath hissed in between his teeth once again, but in a very different way this time, and he rested his forehead against hers, his eyes just dark, blurred pools as they looked deep into hers.

'And I hurled abuse at you—threw you out. *Mi dispiace*—forgive me.'

'You didn't know the whole truth.' Honesty forced her to say it. 'I didn't tell you.'

That made him lift his proud head, burning eyes still locked with hers, his hands curving over the fine bones of her shoulders as he held her slightly away from him.

'Why didn't you tell me?' He gave the question more emphasis than she would ever have expected, the low-toned words almost fierce in their demand.

'Why?'

Emily's head came up, her face pale, the set of her jaw and chin determined, her blue eyes clouded with memory.

'You didn't have the right to know. You judged me without thinking—you condemned me without a trial. And I'd vowed never to share my life with any other man.'

'But you shared my bed—shared your body with me, but you wouldn't share your past, your marriage?'

'It wasn't my secret to share. Mark was ill—dying—and I never told anyone. I never told those who *loved* me. That isn't just sharing—that's intimacy. And we weren't *intimate,* except in one particular way.'

'I see.'

There was a new and very different note in Vito's voice, one that spoke of distance and withdrawal and the very opposite of that intimacy that she had spoken of. And it was only when she heard it that she realised that something else had been in his tone earlier, something that had now vanished completely, leaving his voice cold and heartless without it. Something twisted cruelly in her heart to hear it, a terrible sense of loss. With her realisation of how much she loved this man so fresh in her mind, she felt that so badly that it made her close her eyes against the pain.

'And that physical intimacy is something you regret.'

If possible, Vito's voice was even harder now, making her closed lids fly open in shock and distress.

'Oh, no! No! I don't regret that. Like you, I've never been able to forget our night together. And like you I want that to go on and on until we are sated on each other…'

Which she could never be. It was impossible, unbelievable; she couldn't even begin to imagine that happening. She had only to see him, think of him and she was hungry for him.

'So then why are you keeping your distance from me?'

Why was she? Wasn't the truth that she was punishing herself as much as him? That she was disturbing her nights and making her days long and wearing with the need for him gnawing at her with every second, by denying the wildly blazing attraction that was there between them every second? Even now his closeness, the heady scent of his skin, the touch of his hands on hers was making her pulse throb and cruel hunger uncoil low down in her body, demanding appeasement.

She might not be able to accept his marriage ultimatum, but she could accept this for what it was— simple human need and pleasure in both its most basic and most sophisticated forms, that he could give without commitment and she could give …

…With love.

That thought almost destroyed her, but then Vito's hand moved on hers and her heart leapt again, her pulse rate and the hunger spiking with it, and she could no more have prevented herself from acting on the drumming demand of her senses than she could have stopped herself from breathing.

Leaning forward, she pressed a soft, tentative kiss at the corner of his mouth and knew as soon as the taste of his skin was in her mouth that there was no way she could stop there. Particularly not when she felt and saw that beautifully sensual mouth curl up at the corners before he angled his head towards her and kissed her back.

'I thought you might find me—changed,' she murmured against his mouth, praying that the belief she was embarrassed would give an explanation for the rush of blood to her cheeks, the sudden catch in her breath. 'That you might not think me attractive the way I am now.'

'You cannot be serious.' Vito's voice had thickened noticeably even on the few words. 'You think that I would not like what my child has done to your body? Do you not know that it has made you even more beautiful—more feminine in my eyes?'

'But I—'

'But nothing *carissima—nothing!*'

He punctuated the words with kisses, soft at first then increasing in pressure along the curve of her mouth, the length of her jaw-line.

'You are all I ever wanted in a woman—and all the more so now that you carry my baby. Can you doubt that?'

'I—I...' Emily tried to answer him but the effect that his kisses, his touch was having on her was making her head swim so that she couldn't collect her thoughts, couldn't make her tongue work.

It was as if she had been starving for the long months they had been apart, even the long week of distance she had forced on herself, and now she was presented with the most tempting feast imaginable and told to help herself to what she wanted. His skin was like heated satin under her fingers, his touch a delight that woke further, deeper hungers along every nerve path in her body. His kiss seemed to draw out her soul and take possession of it, taking her heart into his keeping, too, where she knew she would never, ever leave.

'Then let me show you, *tesoro,* let me show you—with my mouth and my hands, with my body—how beautiful you are to me.'

Vito was pushing her back against the pillows as he spoke, kissing her as they went, smoothing the straps of her nightgown down her arms, baring the swell of her breasts to his touch. When he cupped them in his fingers they felt warmer, heavier than ever before and the darker pout of the nipples, the soft tracery of delicate blue veins under the whiteness of her flesh was an enticement to the caress of his mouth, the stroke of his tongue.

'Just tell me that this is safe,' he murmured against her skin, inhaling the warm scent of her body as he spoke. 'Tell me that there is no way that I will harm you or our child…'

If there was then he would have to stop, though God alone knew how he would manage it. Already his hunger was raging out of control, the need to touch, to kiss, to taste overriding all other considerations but…

So it was with a rush of wild relief that he heard her soft laughter, felt it ripple along her body, caught it under his mouth at her throat.

'No risk,' she told him, the warmth of her voice raw-edged with an echo of the hunger he was feeling too. 'None at all.'

It was all he needed. Moments later he had lost himself in the treasures of her body, growing both amazed and delighted by the changes that her pregnancy had created in her. Her breasts were fuller, richer, than ever before, and sensitive— dear God, so sensitive to every touch that she cried out at even the faint drift of his breath over her straining nipples.

Her body too was so much more lush than the

form he had caressed and known five months before, the swell of her belly curving into his hands as if it had been made to fit them perfectly. He smoothed his fingers over the peachy skin, the growing shape of his child within her, and felt the burn of tears at the backs of his eyes as his throat closed up with wild, fierce pride.

He bent his mouth to the precious mound, kissing softly, and could not hold back a cry of pure joy when underneath his lips the baby kicked hard and fast as if in recognition of just who he was and why he was there.

'*Mio bambino,*' he muttered thickly, needing his native Italian for the words, the cold alien sound of English not adequate to express the wonder of it. '*Mio bambino.*'

But then Emily's hands reached for him, pulling him up to her again, her mouth taking his with a hunger that stunned and dazed him, and from the moment that her delicate fingers moved over his skin he was lost, adrift, all control evaporating in the heat of the flames of desire that drove his senses towards total meltdown. Somehow he managed to find enough strength to control his taking of her, to ease himself into her rather than the fierce, driving possession his body craved. But even as he tried to hold himself above her, his forearms taking most of the weight, even as he fought for restraint, Emily was moving underneath him, rubbing herself against him, destroying any hope of further moderation.

With a harsh cry of surrender he gave up the struggle, let her lead him, take from him what she wanted. Her arms imprisoned him, the heated slickness of her femininity enclosed him, and their bodies strained and moved together, yearning, seeking, reaching for the ultimate pleasure that was suddenly so near, so very, very close.

Release came with a ferocity and power that made him feel as if his body was breaking into pieces, shattering like glass. He gathered her up into his arms, enfolded her so tight that he could hardly breathe against her arching form, and with her name on his lips he fell over the top and into the dark abyss of wild, blazing, blinding, total sensual oblivion.

And it was while he still lay against her, sweat-slicked, eyes closed and breathing hard, that he heard her draw in a deep, uneven sigh and speak.

And knew that the words she said were not the ones he wanted to hear at all.

CHAPTER FOURTEEN

'I'LL marry you.'

Emily wasn't even fully aware of having said the words the first time; couldn't be sure that they hadn't just sounded in her head. But when she heard them in her thoughts she knew that they were real, and they were right—they were words she couldn't hold back; words she just had to say. Words that she would never, ever wish undone.

'I've changed my mind. I'll do as you want and I will marry you. I have to marry you. After that, how could I ever marry anyone else?'

It felt so good to have spoken; to have the words out; to have the declaration made. She might not be brave enough to admit how much she loved him, but she had come just as close as she dared. She had told him that she could never marry anyone else and surely that…

But there was something wrong.

It was the silence that got to her first. The silence

that had a dark, shadowed quality about it. And that shadow sent a shivering chill crawling its way over her skin, raising goose-pimples as it passed, making her shiver outwardly—and feel like miserable death deep inside.

'Vito?'

His name was barely a whisper on her lips and she did not dare to open her eyes. His total stillness told her that something was not at all right. And the silence sent out warnings that what she had said was not what he wanted to hear.

'Vito?' she tried again, still hiding behind the concealing shield of her closed eyelids.

'I said I—'

'I know what you said.'

Vito's response was curt, harsh, sounding all the more so because she heard it 'blind', unable to see his face.

'I heard you quite clearly.'

There was a rustle of bedclothes, the sound of movement that told Emily he had slid off the bed, stood up. But still she dared not open her eyes. There was such a terrible, ominous note in his voice that she screwed her eyelids even more tightly shut, suddenly terrified of what she might see if she opened them.

'But I can't accept what you said. I don't want to marry you.'

'You don't?'

This time she couldn't stop herself. Her eyes flew open, looked straight up into the darkness of his. And what she saw there made the nerves in her stomach bunch and twist painfully.

He was standing right beside the bed, looking down at her, but the bleakness in his eyes, the way that mental distance had turned them clouded and opaque made her shiver where she lay. The long, powerful frame that she had just caressed so lovingly, the beautiful body that he had shared with her so intimately was now held stiffly taut, so far away from her that it was as if some transparent screen had come down between them, cutting him off from her. And for all that he was still totally naked, his face was so set and cold that he might have been wearing invisible armour that closed off all his thoughts and feelings from her.

'But you said…'

'I know what I said, but I've changed my mind. I withdraw my proposal.'

'What proposal?'

Fierce, blinding pain drove the sharp question

from her even though every instinct warned that she was blundering into very dangerous territory.

'There was no *proposal,* only the ultimatum that we were getting married whether I liked it or not!'

'Well, then I withdraw that ultimatum.'

If a robot had words, then it would have just those same flat, unmeaning speech patterns. And Vito's eyes had moved away from her face, hunting for something on the floor. When he stooped to snatch up his discarded jeans and pull them on, the brusque, determined movements he used were like a blow to her heart, speaking so eloquently of his rejection of her, the way that the heated passion of the lovemaking they had shared had now evaporated, leaving her body chilled and shivering.

Awkwardly and hesitantly, she reached out for the sheet, struggling to pull it up around her, as much for comfort as concealment. She felt far too vulnerable with Vito's cold, brutal gaze on her naked form.

'And what—what—about the baby? Do you—?'

'Oh, I still want my child,' Vito cut in on her before she could finish the question. 'But as you said, we can work out some arrangement for access. A relationship between us would never work. We would only end up hating each other.'

'Hating each other *more,* you mean!' Emily muttered viciously.

Reaction was setting in hard and fast. She was just beginning to truly realise that while she thought she had been expressing the love she felt for this man, he had in fact just been using her. He'd taken everything she had to give and…

'Well, having nothing but sex between us wouldn't last very long.'

'It didn't last at all!'

Unable to bear the thought of being exposed in any way to those coldly probing eyes, Emily tugged harder on the sheet and coiled it round her tightly, clamping the white cotton close with her folded arms. She was hugging herself for comfort, she knew, struggling to hold herself together, to stop herself from falling apart. Because inside she was breaking apart, splintering into tiny, raw, bleeding pieces so that she felt she would never, ever be whole again.

It would last until he'd had enough, he'd said. *Until I'm sated with you—or you with me. We might have six months; we might have a year…and when it's over I'll tell you straight. No pretence. No lies.*

Well, he'd certainly done that. Whatever else

she could accuse Vito of, there was no doubt that he had kept to his word and told her straight. Absolutely, brutally straight.

'Total honesty,' Emily murmured, remembering. She'd told herself she could take that. She just hadn't thought that all they'd have was *one night.* 'Well, you certainly keep your promises.'

She aimed for a sort of brittle carelessness and missed it by a mile.

'Promises?'

Vito frowned his confusion, not understanding her reference.

'"But I promise you in all the time we are together, I'll never look at another woman, never give you cause to be jealous",' Emily quoted, hiding her pain behind the stiffness of her lips, the cold, clipped tone she used. 'You definitely did that—but then there was hardly enough time for any other woman to appear on the scene.'

'The one thing I can assure you about this...'

Something in the way that Vito spoke, some unexpected note threading through the beautifully accented voice caught on Emily's already agonised nerves, drawing her eyes to his face to see what had changed.

'…Is that there is no other woman—and there will never be now.'

'You can't promise that!'

'Oh, but I can.'

There it was again, that disturbing undertone that tugged at something in her heart, made her need to search his face, to find just what was hidden behind those carefully hooded eyes.

Carefully? Her own choice of adjective brought Emily up sharp, made her pause, made her frown.

Carefully implied deliberate action, deliberate restraint. And deliberate action meant that Vito had planned the response he was making or—rather—planned the response he wanted to show to her. He was not speaking openly, not showing her the truth.

Which meant that the truth was something other than what he was saying.

Emily felt as if her head was spinning, her thoughts tumbling like jigsaw pieces thrown up into the air and she was not at all sure where each one fitted. Suddenly it was as if a new and very different light had been shone on things, making her look again at things she had taken one way.

Was there in fact another way that everything Vito had said, everything he had done, could be interpreted? And if so, how did she find out just which one was real?

'How can you promise that?'

Tentatively, she dipped her toe into the waters of exploring the truth, watching his stunning face closely and seeing the way that his mouth tightened, a muscle jerking in his jaw. Her words had hit home—but in what way?

'No woman will ever come between you and me—now or in the future,' he said, obviously choosing his words with such care that she had the very strong feeling that in some way she didn't quite understand he was actually on the run, backing away from her, with his defences up all around him.

'Well, obviously! Because now you're dumping me and moving on, you're quite free to be with anyone you choose. You've had enough of being intimate with me and you can—'

'No!'

It was the roar of a wounded lion, loud and savage and devastatingly powerful—but ragged all around the edges as if some cruel lash of a whip had driven him to the point of no return.

'No, you're not dumping me?' Emily managed, totally confused. 'I don't understand—because that's what you said—that you don't want to marry me—that a relationship with nothing but sex wouldn't last—'

'Nothing but sex would not be *a relationship,* can't you see that? And how the hell can I ever grow tired of being *intimate* with you when the truth is that that has never happened?'

'It hasn't?'

Emily sank back on the pillows in shock, then just as quickly sat up again as thoughts bombarded her thick and fast—shocking in their potential for what Vito might mean, and devastating in their potential for destruction if he didn't mean what she thought.

'But we… What did we just do here, just now?'

Her rather wild gesture indicated the disarray of the bed around her, her nightdress flung on the floor. Vito's dark eyes followed the wave of her hand very briefly then swung back to her face.

'I believe you have already dismissed that "sharing of our bodies" as not being *intimate* in any real way.'

Did he know what the sharpness of his tone, the flash of something in his eyes gave away? Emily wondered. Vito was *hurting.* Really, genuinely *hurting.* And the way that he quoted a previous conversation back at her gave her the reasons why.

'When I said that we weren't *intimate,* except in one particular way? That matters?'

'It matters.'

It mattered more than he could say, Vito admitted to himself. Something had happened here, in the darkness of the night, in that bed, when he had held Emily and his unborn child in his arms. When he had been able to touch and caress them both, when he had felt them both respond to him. But above all else something had happened when he had made love to her and for the first time ever had known what it felt like to want to be truly intimate—totally intimate with a woman.

'It matters,' he said again. 'Because sharing our bodies is no longer enough.'

He had sex—but that was not what he wanted. Not all he wanted. He wanted that intimacy she had spoken of and without it he now knew that sex alone could never be enough.

'But you said…' Emily began, letting the sentence drop as he turned a blazing glare on her.

'I know what I said—and I know I was a fool to have said it. I thought that I came here to work through this. To have as much of you as I could. To sate myself on you. Get you out of my system. But now …'

He shook his head, despairing at how stupid he had been not to see what was happening to him.

'Now I know that I could never have enough of you. Never ever get you out of my system. I could sleep with you a thousand times—a hundred thousand—and still end up wanting more. Needing more.'

He'd stunned her; that much was obvious. Emily was sitting totally still, blue eyes wide, her soft mouth slightly open.

'Needing…' she echoed huskily, her voice shaking on the single word. 'Needing what?'

'Needing *you.*'

There, now he'd said it. He'd committed himself and there was no going back. Well, there had been no going back anyway, damn it. It was all or nothing—if she didn't want what he wanted, then there was no way he could go on with second best.

'Needing me for sex.'

'*Dannazione,* no—not just for sex!'

This time had been so very different. This time he had felt that true intimacy—at least with his child and, he had thought, with Emily. But if she did not feel that way then he could not go on. He couldn't make love to her—there, that was the difference—he had been *making love* to this woman in a way that he had never, ever done in his life before. No other woman had ever made him feel this way. And because of that he could not continue to *make love* with her if all that it meant to her was just sex. Wonderful, mind-blowing sex—but just sex all the same.

'With other women that might have been enough—might have been all that I wanted. But with you it was just not enough.'

Just not enough. The words echoed over in Emily's thoughts, sounding more wonderful each time she heard them. Vito had never actually said the word 'love' but surely this was as close to a declaration of that feeling as he could possibly get?

'But you thought that I could—that I should marry you just because of the baby. That I could put up with that "not enough".'

Vito sighed, nodded slowly, pushing one hand through the sleek blackness of his hair.

'I did and I was wrong. I realise now that I was trying to tie you down—trying to make you mine without making the real commitment myself. But tonight taught me how wrong I was. When you said you would marry me—that you would accept the little that I'd offered I knew I couldn't go through with it.'

'But you would have got what you wanted.'

'What I thought I wanted, not what I realised tonight that I really wanted. And I couldn't go through life with that longing, that wanting, leaving an empty hole in my heart, a yearning space in my soul. With you, it has to be all or nothing—and if you can't give that all then I have to take the nothing and set you free to be what you want. I would still need to have a connection with you because of the child and I don't know how I am going to cope with that—but that's my problem. I won't ever make any claim on you in the future—I have to let you fly free.'

Her heart was flying now, Emily knew. It was soaring, spinning, dancing in joy at the ardent declaration of love that Vito had made, somehow without ever actually mentioning the word.

'And if I don't want to be free?' she asked softly, the glow in her heart growing even stronger as she saw the way his proud head went back, the stunned look in his deep dark eyes.

'You don't want…?' he echoed, his voice hoarse and raw in a way that made her smile just to hear it. 'But you said that you had vowed never to let a man into your life in that way again.'

'I did—why do you think I said that I couldn't marry you at first? It was because I thought that was all you offered me and I couldn't let that happen again. That was because of Mark. Because he would never let me be free. His form of love was controlling—bullying—we never shared that true intimacy you spoke of. But if you were prepared to set me free because you love me…'

'Love,' Vito echoed softly, a note of something close to awe in his voice. 'Of course. It's such a simple word but it encompasses everything I was trying to say.'

Moving forward, he came to sit down on the bed, taking her hand in his and pressing a long, lingering kiss on the backs of her fingers.

'I love you, Emily. You have my heart and I never, ever want it back.'

'And I love you, Vito Corsentino. I love you and I want to be with you.'

Leaning forward, she pressed her lips to his, felt the catch of his breath against her mouth before he gave himself up to the kiss that said even more than the words he'd given her already. Eventually she drew back with a reluctant sigh. There were things she still needed to make clear.

'I said just now that I would marry you but it

wouldn't have been right—not then—not like it is now. Then I didn't know that you loved me. I thought my love for you would have been enough, but you were right—if I'd married you then, there would have been that hole in my life, in my heart, and I could never have been happy. Now it's all so very different.'

Her smile lit up her whole face, matched the joy that blazed in her eyes.

'Ask me again, Vito. Ask me again so that this time it can be perfect—so that this time we both know what love is and that we can go into the future together.'

The words choked off in her throat as Vito took her hand, looked deep into her eyes and said the words she had dreamed of him saying in just the way that she had longed to hear them.

'Emily, *adorata, tesoro*—I love you and without you my life would be empty, sterile—nothing. Will you marry me and let me spend the rest of my life loving you and sharing with you that true intimacy that only people truly in love can know?'

There was only one answer she could give him, and she couldn't wait to say it, couldn't wait to let him know how happy he had made her.

'Yes, Vito, yes—with all my heart. I can't think of any way I would rather spend my future than sharing it—truly sharing it with you.'

MILLS & BOON PUBLISH EIGHT LARGE PRINT TITLES A MONTH. THESE ARE THE EIGHT TITLES FOR OCTOBER 2007.

THE RUTHLESS MARRIAGE PROPOSAL
Miranda Lee

BOUGHT FOR THE GREEK'S BED
Julia James

THE GREEK TYCOON'S VIRGIN MISTRESS
Chantelle Shaw

THE SICILIAN'S RED-HOT REVENGE
Kate Walker

A MOTHER FOR THE TYCOON'S CHILD
Patricia Thayer

THE BOSS AND HIS SECRETARY
Jessica Steele

BILLIONAIRE ON HER DOORSTEP
Ally Blake

MARRIED BY MORNING
Shirley Jump

Pure reading pleasure

0907 Rom LP

MILLS & BOON PUBLISH EIGHT LARGE PRINT TITLES A MONTH. THESE ARE THE EIGHT TITLES FOR NOVEMBER 2007.

—————— ❦ ——————

BOUGHT: THE GREEK'S BRIDE
Lucy Monroe

THE SPANIARD'S BLACKMAILED BRIDE
Trish Morey

CLAIMING HIS PREGNANT WIFE
Kim Lawrence

CONTRACTED:
A WIFE FOR THE BEDROOM
Carol Marinelli

THE FORBIDDEN BROTHER
Barbara McMahon

THE LAZARIDIS MARRIAGE
Rebecca Winters

BRIDE OF THE EMERALD ISLE
Trish Wylie

HER OUTBACK KNIGHT
Melissa James

MILLS & BOON
Pure reading pleasure